HIGH IRON

Old Hannibal Putnam was a man who just didn't know when he was licked. Not only had he set out to build a railroad on borrowed money, it had to be high up in the hills. And now there's a spy in the camp. Someone who certainly doesn't want a railroad built. Someone who would kill — and has — to stop it. That's when Hannibal decides to send for his former shooting partner, Lefty Malone. Only Lefty hasn't carried a gun in years . . .

E.E. HALLERAN

HIGH IRON

Complete and Unabridged

LINFORD
Leicester

First published in the United States by
Ballantine

First Linford Edition
published 2021
by arrangement with
Golden West Literary Agency

A catalogue record for this book is available
from the British Library.

ISBN 978–1–78541–961–4

Published by
Ulverscroft Limited
Anstey, Leicestershire

Printed and bound in Great Britain by
TJ Books Ltd., Padstow, Cornwall

This book is printed on acid-free paper

1

It took a little over forty minutes for the work train to climb the twelve miles from Fremont Junction to Muleskinner Gulch. Malone spent the time with his sandy beard stuck against a dirty windowpane, pretending an intense interest in the melting snows of the Colorado mountains. To the other passengers in the ancient day coach, he was just another hunter in stained buckskins and shapeless old hat that had once been black. Men looked at the mended saddle on the seat beside him or stared with more interest at the muzzle of the big Sharps buffalo gun that jutted out of the blanket roll in the overhead rack. No one seemed to notice that the ragged hat brim was always adjusted to an angle that permitted keen gray eyes to keep sharp watch on the people in the car.

When the train began to buck and clank against unevenly applied brakes, there was a stir of action among the laborers, gamblers, and adventurers who partly filled the coach. They reached for carpetbags, slicker rolls, leather valises, and gunny sacks, all of them eager to get out for a look at the railhead camp at Muleskinner. The biggest show of activity, however, was around the four shrill women who bad been entertaining visitors all the way up from Fremont. At the first hint that the train was nearing the end of its run, they had begun to adjust gaudy bonnets, straighten false hair, and smooth rumpled gowns. They had also done a lot of giggling as the jerking of the train gave them excuses to fall into the arms of their male admirers-and gave the male admirers opportunities to give them something to giggle about.

Malone was mildly amused by the performance, but he remembered the part he had to play. He even let the hat brim come down an inch as he saw the look that was being aimed at him by the redheaded woman who seemed to be the ramrod of the female contingent. Tillie Atherton was curious. She had been curious ever since leaving Fremont Junction. Malone hoped that nothing more than curiosity would come into those hard green eyes. It would be awkward to have Tillie getting too brilliant with her memories. He turned to study the mud and slush again, now having something more to see. The train was jolting to a halt beside rows of stacked rails and freshly hewn ties. Up ahead were immense stacks of boxes and kegs which would contain such items as spikes and fishplates. Everything was just as Hannibal Putnam had told him it would be. During the winter months the Silverdale and Fremont had used its original twelve miles of track to good advantage, hauling in as much material as possible for the big push up Muleskinner Gulch and across the mountains to Silverdale. Old Put had planned and organized well; it was no fault of his that other troubles were threatening.

And the troubles were real, Malone now felt sure. He had been skeptical at first about the talk of hostile Utes and belligerent freight-line operators, but the past forty minutes had told him plenty. A man like Carl Grimes didn't show his face in a place like this unless somebody was paying for the kind of dirty work that was his specialty. The mere sight of Grimes at Fremont Junction had warned Malone that there was a real job ahead.

Grimes was alone now, getting his luggage together, but all the way up the winding track from Fremont he had been moving about in the car, visiting and gossiping with the men Putnam had hired and sent up to the construction camps. Twice Malone had heard samples of the smooth Grimes style as the little man spoke unhappily about the Ute problem. Grimes was getting down to work in a hurry, reminding construction workers of the dangers they would face if they went to work for the railroad company.

Malone wasted no time on admiring the Grimes technique. He already knew that the round-faced little man was practically a genius at the job of sowing discontent among laborers. Usually his line was to sympathize with men because they were underpaid or badly treated, but this time he had a different approach. Not that the topic made any difference. The important point was that Carl Grimes was on the job. Somebody had hired him to put on his act.

That much had become clear to Malone before the train had even left Fremont Junction. Then he had spotted another familiar figure a few seats ahead of him. Jim Hatfield was a gunfighter whose skill was always up for hire. Hatfield and Grimes had been on opposite sides in more than one bit of frontier trouble, so it seemed a little suspicious that they should now be in the same railroad car — ignoring each other. Malone decided promptly that the pair had to be tied up in some way. It was too much of a strain on the imagination to assume that the Silverdale and Fremont had two separate lots of enemies. For Malone, this meant an extra complication. Hatfield might possibly do some remembering. Like Tillie Atherton, he might see something familiar in the lean face behind the sandy whiskers.

It took a long time for Malone to pick up the hint he expected, but finally it came. Hatfield had been sleeping, doubled up into the shabby plush seat with his expensive brown hat tipped to the bridge of his long nose. He had taken no part in the scare talk that occupied those workmen who were not more concerned with the women up front. He hadn't even looked around when Grimes began to move about the car with his careful, prodding conversation. It was Grimes, not Hatfield, who finally showed the hand. The little man had just left the noisy crowd at the front of the car and was lurching back down the aisle, his derby hat shoved to the back of his round head so that the cherubic smile that was so much his stock-in-trade could have its full effect. Suddenly his smile changed just a little and he glanced straight at Hatfield. Malone could see the brief jerk of tho gunman's hat brim, and then Grimes nodded and went past. It wasn't much, but it was enough for Malone. The pair had some kind of understanding. Who ever was trying to stir up trouble for the railroad had picked a fine set of trouble-makers as agents.

As the train grated to a final, shuddering halt, the Grimes campaign was already showing its effects. In the comparative quiet Malone heard a burly workman growl, 'They better have plenty guards on this job. I ain't riskin' them goddam Utes less'n we got somebody lookin' after us.'

A companion muttered uneasily in reply, 'We take a look. If'n it Jiggers too risky, we kin git out.'

Hatfield came up out of his seat, towering over the two men. 'Always another job, gents,' he declared amiably. 'I represent the new crowd what's takin' over the wagon business up here. We'll need good men — and it seems like the Utes ain't got no crow to pick with the wagon outfits. We ain't haulin' through their Manitou country like the railroad's

7

fixin' to do. Look me up if'n you git too damned spooked up about the Injun raids.' He made it sound as though there definitely would be raids.

It gave Malone a new angle to consider. Hatfield didn't sound like the same old gunman. He spoke with authority, and his talk of a new company in the freight business hinted that he was holding more cards than usual in this deal. Maybe it really was the freight-wagon interests that had been starting all those rumors about Indian threats. The wagoners would keep the hauling trade only until the rail line went through. Possibly they hoped to scare away construction workers and to keep the railroad from taking over as long as they possibly could.

Putnam had not been too sure about any of it. That was why he had sent Malone in. Simply starting rumors wouldn't be the last of it if the wagon outfits — or anyone else — really wanted to block construction. It would be Malone's job to handle any more violent efforts on the part of the opposition.

Hatfield followed the two work-men toward the rear door, avoiding the hilarious crowd that was escorting the women in the opposite direction. Malone had a moment to hear Grimes joining in Hatfield's remarks — talking like a stranger — before he saw Tillie Atherton staring at him again. It didn't seem likely that Tillie would have any professional interest in a dirty old mountain man, so he had to assume that her curiosity was the result of partial recognition. He thought he would continue to sit and stare out the window, but he quickly real-ized that it would only make him more conspicuous. He had to join the others who were leaving the car.

Taking the bold course suggested something else. He looked straight at Tillie and gave her a big grin, smiling broadly as he did so. She turned away at once and let a hulking workman escort her out to the car's platform. That was the ticket, Malone thought. Making a pass at Tillie was the very best thing he could do. Such a move would never

9

remind her of the man she might be close to recognizing.

He felt quite pleased with himself when he lifted the blanket roll out of the rack and picked up the saddle with his other hand. He felt good about remembering to squint when he leered at Tillie. It wouldn't have been smart to let her get a real good look at his eyes. Once, people had commented that his gray eyes could be just as hard as Tillie's green ones, and he didn't want anything to remind her of it.

Maybe the whole incident had been to the good. It was a reminder that he had to be careful about small things. When a man is trying to look twenty years older than he is, he has to watch the details.

From the rear platform of the coach, he could see a huddle of buildings across the narrow valley. One big log structure was the center of a tangle of corrals, sheds, and cabins of all sizes. That would be the freighter outfit's headquarters. Wagons and pack horses had been taking in supplies and bringing out high-grade ore ever since the Silverdale mines went into operation. Because they needed to double their teams for the haul over the pass, they had set up a relay station here at the mouth of Muleskinner Gulch, and in two years it had become quite a town. There would be a lot of people who wouldn't want it to become a ghost town.

Malone went down the car steps to join the crowd huddled along the track, taking turns at using the line of planking that spanned the mud to where a regular plank walk had been constructed. Passengers from the other end of the car had claimed precedence, and there was plenty of rough ceremony in getting Tillie and her girls across.

Malone let a couple of workmen shoulder hiill aside, and once more he felt pretty good about the way he was acting. There had been a time when he might have knocked both of them into the mud hole, but now he was supposed to be a harmless old fellow who wasn't interested in anything except getting back into the hills, away from people.

The delay gave him a chance to take a look at the temporary buildings the Silverdale and Fremont had thrown up as their railhead camp. All along the track were corrals and sheds, some of them mere shelters for the more perishable materials being gathered there, but others more solidly built. He could identify an office, several shacks evidently built to house workmen, and a couple of slab warehouses. There was nothing in sight that could not be torn down in a hurry when those final twenty miles of rail reached across the high country to the Silverdale mines.

He saw that Grimes and Hatfield were walking together now, following the women and their escorts to the buildings across the valley. Other men were turning to follow the plank walk toward what appeared to be the local office of the railroad. He followed the latter group but did not turn in at the office with them. As soon as all the passengers had gotten out of the single coach, the engineer had started up again, the puffing of the distant engine throwing black smudges on the remaining patches of dirty snow. A break in the train suggested that some cars were to be drilled off on another siding, and Malone wanted to make sure that he claimed the saddle horse that was in one of the boxcars before some thickhead got the animal mixed up with the company's draft horses. There was no point in calling unnecessary attention to himself by getting mixed up in any such tangle as that.

He ambled along past the flatcars which had been left with the coach, noting that they were loaded with the new tilt-up carts, which railroad graders were using so efficiently. In front of them were gondolas with more ties and rails. Old Put was doing everything possible to get the job done.

They were getting the first mules out of a boxcar when he reached the corral area. A fat man in corduroy pants and a big buffalo coat was arguing loudly with the lanky stoop-shouldered fellow who seemed to be bossing the job. It was a friendly-sounding argument in spite of its violence, and Malone thought he could detect a hint of humor in the lanky man's growl.

'Dammit, Matt, there ain't no point in palaverin' wid me about it. Ye're the boss man around here, but ye've still got to git the papers from the office.' The words came in a colorful mixture of Irish brogue and Southwestern drawl.

'I know all about the damned papers, ye skinny bastard,' the fat man retorted. 'All I'm askin' is that ye pick out the six best critters in the lot and hold 'em fer me. Don't let none o' them graders o' yourn hide 'em out on me!' The nasal voice was curiously high-pitched, loud enough so that the hostlers working with the mules were grinning in appreciation.

The lanky man nodded, evidently not concerned over the lanuage being used on him. 'So git the paper from Wheeler. I got to have . . .'

'Hell! I know that! Jest hold onto them big brutes fer me. I'll git the paper from

14

Wheeler if I have to wring his scrawny neck.'

The stoop-shouldered man's grimace showed broken teeth. 'Could be a real good idea — but mebbe ye'd better git the paper from Miss Isabel. She's got sense enough to know why ye need the mules.'

The fat man laughed. 'Hell of a railroad. Even a goddam mule nurse knows that a woman's runnin' it.'

'Git movin',' the lanky one advised amiably. 'Mebbe a mite of action could work some o' the lard off'n yer fat butt. Seems like the bossier ye are the fatter ye git.'

The round man cursed him cheerfully, then swung to face Malone. For a full minute he said nothing, the broad face taking on a completely blank expression. It was the little eyes peering out from behind fat cheeks and bushy brows that warned that the man was making a careful appraisal of the tall stranger. Malone knew that the fat man was missing nothing, and he was glad that this was not an

15

old acquaintance he was facing. A crop of sandy whiskers wouldn't fool this fellow very long.

'Lookin' fer me?' the fat man asked finally, his voice still loud enough to be heard halfway across the little valley. Apparently his normal tone was something between a bellow and a roar.

'Maybe I could be a bit later,' Malone admitted. 'Right now I'm aimin' to get my horse away from your muleskinners before they bitch him to one of them dump wagons.'

A pudgy hand indicated the lanky man. 'Talk to Flannery. He's the straw boss fer mules and sech. But if'n ye're plannin' to talk to me about anything, ye'd best do it now. I git real busy.'

'Suits me,' Malone agreed. 'You're Matt Terpin, I take it?'

'Ye take it right. How'd ye know?'

Malone let an easy smile crinkle the whiskers. 'Hannibal Putnam told me about you — and your voice. Not likely to be any mistake, I reckon. And I heard Flannery call you Matt.' He reached into the buckskin jacket and brought out a folded bit of paper, which he handed to Terpin. 'From Old Put.'

Terpin pushed it away. 'I ain't a readin' man, and I don't fool around with excuses about leavin' my readin' glasses in my Sunday vest. What's the danmed thing say?'

'It says that I'm to report at your upper camp and start providing it with meat. I'm to have a pack horse and ammunition. Beyond that I'm on my own. I get paid for meat — deer, elk, or bear — at the going price for regular beef at Fremont Junction. I bring the kill to your camp and take a receipt for its weight. Your men dress it out.'

Terpin's nod suggested that the idea appealed to him, but then the frown came back. 'Sounds to me like ye took old man Putnam real good on that deal. The comp'ny supplies a hoss and ammunition, likewise skinners and butchers. Yuh git full beef price. How'n hell did yub git him to swaller a deal like that?'

'It's a good deal — for both sides,'

Malone told him. 'Mr. Putnam knows that providing a horse and ammunition would be cheaper than buying beef and having it hauled across the mountains. You need all of your stock for grading chores; you can't afford to waste them on hauling beef to that other camp of yours.'

'Mebbe yuh're right about that part But what makes yuh think yuh're smart enough to supply a hundred hardeatin' men with meat? That's how many we'll have up there if we kin git 'em.'

Malone shrugged. 'No supply, no pay. I aim to get paid.'

The frown remained as the fat man turned to shout an order at Flannery. 'See about this varmint's boss, Denny. I don't want him to have no excuse fer not handlin' his job.'

'Chestnut with three white feet,' Malone added. 'Branded reverse LM connected.'

Flannery looked around with a puzzled expression on his lean face. 'Lemme hear that again, mister. It didn't make much sense to me.' Then he let one eyelid droop a little as he added solemnly, 'Could be I didn't hear ye all the way through. After a man has had his ears blasted by a fat steam whistle, it's kinda hard to hear ordinary noises what human people make.'

'Aw, go to hell!' Terpin roared. 'I ain't no louder'n . . . '

Malone didn't want to waste the opportunity to identify himself in the style he preferred. 'My own brand,' he broke in loudly. 'M with a spur on the bottom left to make a backwards L. LM for Lefty Malone. That's me.'

Flannery nodded and went back to bossing his crew. Terpin motioned toward one of the warehouses that flanked the corrals. 'Git on over there and stash yer gear. It'll be safe. Then we kin go take care o' yer business. I'm kinda curious to see what Miss Isabel is gonna say about that cockeyed contract o' yourn.'

2

Malone knew that Terpin was watching his every move as he disposed of the war bag and saddle. Maybe it was just as well to have things work out like this, even though he hadn't planned to push matters quite so fast. He knew that Hannibal Putnam was depending pretty heavily on five key people for the actual operation here in the mountains. While old Put had to spend so much of his time in Denver and similar cities, worrying about financing the job, he had to trust those five with everything. And not only was Terpin the most important figure in the group, he was also the most questionable.

It wasn't that Putnam had been under any illusions about the man. Terpin's reputation — or his variety of reputations — was public property. He was a loud-mouthed braggart who could be backed down by any man with a little guts. He was a liar. He was a scoundrel who had been involved in any number of crooked games, mostly saving his own skin by double-crossing his partners. And he was probably the best construction boss in the West. Putnam had gambled on Terpin the crook in order to get Terpin the grading boss.

'Let me do the talkin' at the office,' the fat man suggested a bit pompously. 'It'll take less time that way.' His tone seemed to have changed. Minutes earlier he had made it sound almost like a threat to suggest taking Malone to the company's office. Now he appeared to feel that it was a routine matter that he wanted to help along.

'Sounds like you ain't so sure but what it's a good deal,' Malone commented.

'It's a good deal,' Terpin agreed. 'But I ain't so goddam sure that yuh're what yuh claim. That part I aim to find out about later.'

'What else would I be?' Malone inquired. He made it sound casual, almost innocent, hoping to get something in the way of real information from the fat man.

Terpin obliged. 'It's this way, Mister Lefty Malone. We got a railroad to build, and some sonsabitches is tryin' to stop us. Right now we ain't sure who's back o' the trouble. Mebbe wagon outfits, mebbe Injuns, mebbe somebody we don't even know about. The point is, and ye'd better git it into yer head, that this here's kind of a funny company. I got stock in it. So's Flannery. Most o' the crew's takin' stock fer part o' their wages. We got plenty reason to see that no bastard tries to bust us up.'

Malone swallowed his anger. Putnam hadn't told him about the stock deal. Now he had to start making estimates all over again. Or maybe it just wasn't true. A liar like Terpin might tell such a thing to a stranger, assuming that the stranger couldn't check up on him.

'I kinda think we'll get along,' Malone said finally. 'One of the things Old Put asked me to do was to keep my eyes open while I was huntin'. Maybe he had Indians in mind but I kinda doubt it.'

'Yuh better not be plannin' no dirty work,' Terpin growled. 'I'll bust yuh wide open my own self. Here's the office. Shut up and let me do the talkin'!'

They went in under the sign neatly lettered OFFICE in red and gold. It was obviously the product of the same hand that had put those artistic gold letters on the wheezing little locomotive and the ancient day coach that the company used to haul its labor force and a few passengers. At least the Silverdale and Fremont had a good sign painter on its payroll.

The log building was all one room, but a counter formed a half partition across its middle. At one end a sallow-looking man was checking in the last of the new workmen who had come up on the train. The other end seemed to be the business office. There, another sallow man occupied a desk that almost blocked the doorway. On the desk was another neatly lettered sign. It said that he was Mr. J. T. Withers, Chief Clerk.

Terpin ignored the sign, the desk, and

Mr. Withers. He pushed past into the middle of the room, pausing halfway between another pair of desks. The one with the trim brunette behind it carried the tag MISS PUTNAM. The one in the corner where a lean, sleek-haired man worked over a sheaf of papers carried a sign of the same size. It read, Mr. Mark Wheeler, Chief of Supply.

'Got a bit o' business fer yuh, Miss Isabel,' Terpin bawled in what he seemed to think was a courteous tone.

Miss Putnam looked up, a half smile quirking the corners of a mouth that had its attractive features. Malone decided that Hannibal Putnam must have had a pretty wife. Certainly his daughter had picked up a lot of charm and beauty that she had never gotten from her old man.

'Did you need to come here with your errand, Mr. Terpin?' she asked in a mild voice.

'Sure, ma'am. It's . . .'

'I don't care what it is!' The voice had lost its mildness. She was practically barking at the fat man now. 'With the

24

tone you use, you don't need to come here at all. Just yell it out from somewhere back in the mountains. I'll hear you — and so will everybody else!'

Terpin didn't seem to be annoyed. 'So I'm a mite loud,' he agreed. 'Sorta gits to be a habit, all the time hollerin' at pick and shovel men — and with mules soundin' off and . . . '

She laughed then, smooth oval features seeming to change with the expression. First, she had been a serious worker with only a little trace of smile hinting that there might be feeling behind those perfect features. Then the laugh changed it all. Malone decided that her features weren't really perfect at all. They were simply attractive. Or maybe cute was the word he wanted to use.

By the time he had it figured out, the moment was over. She sobered once more, and some of the snap came back into her voice as she asked, 'What was it you wanted, Matt?' At least she wasn't being formal about it.

'Mules, ma'am. Six of 'em. That fool

Flannery wants a paper before he'll turn 'em over to me.'

Wheeler spoke for the first time. He didn't even turn his head to look at Terpin, but his dry, almost sarcastic voice said, 'Requisition papers are necessary for all such cases. You certainly understand that, Mr. Terpin.'

Terpin's voice also changed. He had been slyly humorous with Miss Putnam, but now there seemed to be no expression in his tone. 'I know it. That's how come I'm here. I want the papers to git six o' them mules what come up on the train today.' Then he added with just a hint of sarcasm, 'I left it here to git signed two days ago.'

That started a brisk conversation between Wheeler and Withers. The clerk had the requisition. He had left it on Wheeler's desk, but it had been returned unsigned. Nobody seemed to know very much about any part of it.

Miss Putnam broke in on the flow of talk. 'What difference does it make how the paper became mislaid?' she demanded sharply. 'The point is that Mr. Terpin needs the mules. Get the requisitions through!'

Wheeler stared with open distaste at the fat man, then turned his sleek head just a few degrees and looked at Isabel, the slight movement making a big difference in both his expression and his tone. 'Aren't we being a trifle hasty Isabel?' he murmured. 'It seems to me that this is not the time to be taking work animals away from Flannery. He needs every bit of help we can give him.'

Malone was alert to every shade of expression. On his mental list of key personnel Terpin had the top spot, but Isabel Putnam and Mark Wheeler would have to rate close behind. Between them they were responsible for the endless details involved in keeping construction crews supplied. Old Put had been a bit apologetic at having sent his daughter in to do a man's work, but he had explained that she wanted to help. Having been at school in the East during most of the time that her father had prowled the mountains as a prospector, she did not have exactly the type of training to fit her for the job here at Muleskinner, but she was smart and she was loyal. Under the circumstances, Putnam had decided to gamble on her. Wheeler was the man who had had experience with the problems of supply.

Now Malone wondered. Wheeler's tone hinted that the office team had become pretty cordial.

Miss Putnam returned the smile that had been aimed toward her. 'I agree,' she said. Then her voice became crisp again. 'But I also recall that we discussed Matt's need for the mules. Find that requisition and put it through.'

Wheeler's face fell. He practically jammed his eyeglasses onto his nose and came out from behind his desk to go into conference with the meek little Mr. Withers.

Terpin didn't waste time crowing over his victory. He promptly repeated what Malone had told him and asked for additional requisitions for the horse, food, and ammunition. Only then did Miss Putnam swing around to take a good look at the tall man in the dirty buckskins. Malone liked the cool way she did it. Old Put hadn't made any mistake in putting this young woman on the job.

'My father hired you?' she asked quietly.

He nodded, handing over the note that Terpin had turned back to him. She read it and asked almost the same question that Terpin had asked. 'How did you persuade my father to agree to such terms as those?'

Again Malone explained the economics of the deal. She listened carefully, brown eyes staring straight past Malone now as she concentrated. He decided that he liked the eyes almost as much as he had liked her laughter. It was something else that he would have to be careful about; he couldn't afford to get interested in any woman, particularly this one.

'I suppose it's all right,' she agreed finally. 'My father usually knows what he's doing.'

'Sometimes I'm not so sure,' Wheeler interrupted, turning back to his desk with some papers in his well-manicured hands. 'I understood that O'Boyle was already planning to feed his men by hunting. This seems like a duplication of service.'

'This'll keep men on their reg'lar jobs,' Terpin said in surprisingly quiet tones. 'I reckon I'd rather trust Old Put's judgment than somebody else's that I know.' He didn't even look toward Wheeler as he spoke, but clearly nobody doubted his meaning.

There was an interval of silence while the necessary forms were completed, and then Miss Putnam turned to Terpin once more. 'What about the powder, Matt? Did you get it?'

'On today's train, ma'am. Forwarded straight to me, so I don't need no papers outa this office. That's why I need the mules. We won't save no time on that blastin' job if'n we don't git it done right away. Reg'lar grade work will be gettin' started in another day or two if the snow keeps meltin'.'

Miss Putnam didn't look toward Malone again, and presently he followed Terpin out into the warm April sunshine. It occurred to him that he had now had a good look at four of the five people he needed to know. Isabel Putnam was supposed to be her father's personal representative while the old man was busy elsewhere. Malone thought she was doing pretty well at it. Terpin was the actual construction boss, and he seemed to know what he wanted. Flannery might be all right in his job bossing the main grading crew. Wheeler was an open question; Malone didn't like him, and he wasn't sure why. Maybe the man's evident taste for red tape was all right for a fellow in his kind of work.

Outside the office, Terpin turned to stare hard at Malone. 'Better cut out the fancy act, mister,' he said, his voice a husk that he evidently thought was a whisper. 'Yuh're up to somethin'. What is it?'

'I already told you. I don't . . . '

'Don't lie to me. Back there yuh put on a real old mountain tone when yuh talked to Miss Isabel. A spell ago yuh sounded damned near educated. I don't like polecats what put on no act around me.'

Malone chuckled, partly to hide his own chagrin. He had promised himself to be careful about those little details, but already he had slipped. 'With you I don't put on any act,' he explained. 'But that Wheeler galoot sounded a bit hard to please, so I thought I ought to sound like a mountain man. Anything wrong with that?'

'Mebbe not. And there better not be! Yuh heard what I said before we went in there. It still goes.'

'And my answer still goes. But what's all this rush for mules and blasting powder? I understood that you wouldn't be getting down to real work for another ten days or so.'

'Snow's goin'. Mebbe we start work a mite sooner. But that's not the point.

32

Did Old Put tell yuh about how we're-workin' from both ends?'

'Sure. That's the point of havin' another camp that needs to be supplied with meat.'

'So we got a crew workin' up the grade outa Silverdale valley. They ain't goin' to lay no rail, but they'll git the gradin' done so that when they meet the main outfit we'll save a lot o' time. Won't take long to put the rail down once the grade's ready fer 'em.'

'I understand that part.'

'Shut up and let me tell it my way. Anyhow, the other camp ain't goin' to git movin' quite as soon as this one. Snow's deeper up there, and it ain't goin' to melt off so soon. We know that there's a couple o' bad bits o' rock on the line they'll be workin', so I figgered to git the blastin' done before the gradin' crew gits there. Snow won't hold up the blast job, and we'll save ourselves a lot o' lost time. Got the idea?'

'I got it. Now, where do I get my pack horse and the ammunition?'

'Ask Flannery about the hoss. I ain't sure about the shells. Could be there won't be any on hand. That buffalo gun o' yourn ain't a real popular size in these parts. Likely yuh'll have to git ammunition sent in.'

'One more thing. How would it be if I ride up to the camp with the powder wagon? Might as well get the lay of the land and have somebody to guide me in. After that I reckon I'll find my way around all right.'

'Yuh'll be a hell of a hunter if yuh can't. Be ready to shove off in the mornin'. I'm goin' up with the powder and I'll take yuh across along our right-of-way. Sorta show yuh how the rail line's supposed to go. Mebbe yuh'll git the idea about how come we got all this talk about rail goin' through Injun country.'

'I've already got that idea,' Malone said. 'It's a lot of scare talk to keep workmen from taking jobs with you.'

'How do yuh know?'

'Take my word for it. You figured it that way yourself, didn't you?'

'Yep. But I'd like to be able to pin it on somebody.'

'So would I. Right now I can't.'

'Then go git yer hoss from Flannery. I ain't needin' no more talk.'

The fat man turned in at one of the storage sheds, and Malone went on along the track toward the corrals. He hadn't taken a dozen strides when he heard men singing ahead of him. Then he saw them. A crew of some twenty hard case characters were coming down the slope of the mountain that blocked the end of the valley. There was a graded path there, evidently the start of what would be a continuation of the rail line. Most of the snow was gone at that point, and Malone assumed that these men had been doing a little work in preparation for the big job that would start as soon as the ice was out of the ground. It seemed pretty clear that neither Terpin nor Flannery would waste any time. For Malone, both men were about to be crossed off the suspect list. Terpin's reputation was an odd one, but on this job he seemed to be playing a straight game.

He began to pick up some of the words that the men were singing as they marched along in almost military style. No one seemed to be giving them any orders or attempting to keep them in line, so Malone assumed that this was the hard core of Flannery's work gang. These men had developed a spirit of their own. It was a point worth remembering.

He recognized the tune as one he had often heard in saloons back in Kansas, where it had been popular with track gangs on other construction jobs. The Irish seemed to enjoy singing the songs that had been intended to make fun of them.

Wid me philalloo, hubbaboo, whack
    hurroo, boys,
Didn't we sing 'til our jaws did ache,
And shout and laugh and drink an
    sing,
Oh, it's lots of fun at Flannery's wake.

The men were closing in on him before he straightened it out in his mind. The song was really called *Finnegan's Wake*, but the men had evidently substituted Flannery's name for Finnegan. The verse that they shouted as they approached the bunk house dealt with a railroad boss who slept with the mules until the mules wouldn't put up with him any longer. Even in the rowdiest of the Kansas saloons, Malone had never heard those words. Flannery's men were having fun at the expense of their boss. It was a good sign. These men were not going to cause any trouble.

Terpin's voice sounded at Malone's shoulder as the work crew broke ranks. The fat man had an uncanny knack of moving around soundlessly. 'Too damned bad we ain't got a hunnert like 'em. Denny's got hisself a good lot and so does O'Boyle up at the other camp — but we ain't gittin' near enough help fer 'em.'

'You're no ready for full crews yet, are you?' Malone asked.

'Any day now. We oughta have 'em here. I'd send fifty up to O'Boyle right now if'n we could git 'em in here. Old Put ain't movin' very fast with his hirin'.'

'Maybe he's having trouble. There's a lot of talk about the Utes. Men could be scared to hire on.'

'Hell! That Injun talk don't amount to nothin'! Any man with a grain o' sense knows that the Utes ain't no problem.'

'Sure — but how many brilliant men are you expecting to hire for your pick and shovel jobs? Any jigger dumb enough to try shoveling a narrow gauge line through these mountains is stupid enough to believe almost anything. And a lot of people are talkin' up that Indian business.'

'Who?' Terpin's expression changed with his tone. 'That's what I want to know. What goddam bastard is doin' this talkin'?'

'A man named Grimes, for one. He was soundin' off real strong on the train today. I think maybe he hired away some of the men Old Put sent up for your gangs. There was a man named Hatfield on the car, also. He made it clear that the wagon outfits would hire any men who didn't like the risk of working for the railroad.'

Terpin cursed briskly for a full minute. Then he aimed a suspicious stare at Malone. 'How come yuh know the names o' them polecats? Was they tryin' to talk yuh out o' bein' a meat hunter?'

Malone grinned. 'They ignored me. But I overheard some of the talk — and I've seen both Grimes and Hatfield before. They didn't recognize me, but I recognized them. You happen to know either of 'em?'

'Carl Grimes.' The name came out bitterly. 'I heard of the bastard. Who's payin' him?'

'That's what I'd like to know. I think maybe I'll wander across to the freight settlement this evening and do some snooping. Maybe I'll pick up an idea or two.'

'Yuh'll have time fer it,' Terpin told him. 'I ain't takin' that powder wagon up tomorrer like I planned. Got to stick around here till I make sure that Denny's got enough men to start work. Powder kin wait a day while we hear what kind of message Miss Isabel gits from her pappy. She sent him word about hurryin' along more men.'

'Suits me,' Malone said quietly. 'I ain't in any hurry.'

Terpin turned to stare hard at him. Since he was practically as tall as Malone, the staring match was a fairly even proposition, angry little eyes against steady gray ones. 'One thing, mister. I know about this here Grimes and how he works. If you're workin' fer him, yuh sonofabitch, I'll kill yuh! I might kill yuh even if'n I git a suspicion that yuh're workin' fer him.'

'You're a damned fool to tell me that,' Malone said evenly. 'But I guess we understand each other — and Carl Grimes.'

3

Terpin's tone changed abruptly. 'Make yerself at home over there in the warehouse. Come along and I'll show ye. Cots in a pile back o' some canned goods. Git yerself fixed up any way ye like. It'll be better'n tryin' to sleep in the bunk shack with them singin' apes o' Flannery's.'

Malone followed him into a building where supplies had been piled in some profusion. There was a heavy bunk built into a front corner, a pile of gear, a rifle and saddle near its head. Evidently this was Terpin's quarters. The fat man didn't trust the flimsy cots provided by the company.

'I hope you don't talk in your sleep,' Malone remarked. 'Not in your regular tone anyway. I'd rather hear the apes.' He was heading toward the supply of cots as he spoke, leaving Terpin to curse him from the rear. At least this job was going to have its entertaining moments.

When he was set up for the night, he took time to wash off some of the train dirt, being careful not to look too neat. For a little while he wanted to continue with his role of hunter.

'Supper's about due,' Terpin told him. 'Want to come along?'

'No. I think I'll eat over in Wagon Town. Seems like there ought to be some kind of hotel or saloon there. Women don't move in unless they've got a place like that to do business.'

'Suit yerself,' Terpin growled. 'But remember what I told ye!'

Before Malone could reply, there was a sharp rap at the slab door and Miss Putnam's voice called out, 'All right for me to come in, Matt?'

The fat man took a hasty glance around the place and bellowed, 'Come right ahead, ma'am. We're all neat and proper.'

To Malone's surprise, two women entered the building, Miss Putnam followed by a little old lady in a black dress that would have seemed more appropriate at a sewing bee in Ohio. Malone was so surprised that at first he didn't see the stern frown that the younger woman was wearing.

'My aunt, Miss Putnam,' the girl announced briskly. 'I suppose my father told you that he couldn't trust me up here in the mountains without a chaperone.' There was no mistaking the bitterness in her voice.

'Seems like he failed to tell me a lot of things,' Malone said, not quite sure of himself. 'But I'm pleased to know you, ma'am.' He decided that the introduction had not been needed. The little old lady was Old Put's sister, right enough. She looked like him.

'And he failed to tell me a few things!' the younger woman snapped. 'He didn't tell me that he was going to send someone in to take charge.'

Malone heard Terpin's angry grunt, but then the girl hurried on. 'I had a letter from him today. I hadn't read it when you were at the office, so I permitted myself to be deceived by your silly disguise. Now I think we should start being honest with each other.'

Terpin's voice rose in a shout. 'I knowed the bast — the polecat had somethin' crooked about him! Want me to start bustin' him up, Miss Iz?'

Her smile was fleeting. 'You'd better listen and stop talking, Matt. This is Mr. Arthur Malone. He is my grand old parent's partner, and he has come up here to see that we don't make too many mistakes. Apparently my father has decided that a woman isn't capable of handling routine duties!'

'You've got it wrong,' Malone told her. 'I don't know what Hannibal put into that letter, but I'm not going to interfere with anybody, you or Matt or anybody else. Let's get that clear right away.'

'Then why all this silly disguise?' She wasn't asking for information; she was challenging him.

'Better sit down,' he advised. 'It's a long yarn, and I reckon I'd better tell it all. This is no time for any of us to be rawhiding each other. We've got enough other people to fight without wrangling among ourselves.'

The older woman steered her companion across to Terpin's cot. The pair of them perched on its edge, waiting.

'It's like this,' Malone explained. 'Hannibal Putnam and I were partners in a prospect hole up in Montana. Once we found out we had something real good, he left me to develop it. That was three years ago. I've been there ever since, leaving him to go on with the kind of prospecting that he liked. You know what happened up in the valley. He hit it big, and it became Silverdale. I've never seen the place, but I kept hearing about it from Hannibal,' mostly because he wanted me to know that the whole thing was a part of our partnership deal. We understood each other. I took care of the Montana property, and he began to go big with this one. We even used Montana profits to start this railroad project.'

'He implied something of the sort,' she admitted. 'I'm not questioning your right. I'm just annoyed that you should come up here in such a sneaky fashion, not trusting any of us.'

'I suppose it sounds bad. We didn't mean it that way. I had a letter from Hannibal about the time I was selling out the Montana diggings. He said he had troubles here but he couldn't find out what kind of troubles he had. When I showed up looking like I do now — after a winter in the mountains — he suggested that I come along and play up this contract hunter business.'

'Then he doesn't trust any of us?'

'Whoa, lady! Stop being sore and start thinking. Your father's got troubles. He knows that his finances are pretty tight. If he gets this rail line working by the middle of the summer and can start bringing out some of the ore that's been piling up at Silverdale, he'll be in the clear. If the line doesn't start paying by mid-August, he's going to have a lot of creditors breathing down his neck. Now, it seems as though somebody — and we don't know who — is out to delay construction.'

'Of course. Those wagon people have

been making a nice profit out of hauling supplies in and high-grade ore out. They don't want us to break up their neat little package.'

'Maybe it's as simple as that. Then again, maybe it's not. Anyhow, we decided that I'd come up here and play stupid while I took a good look around.'

'Spyin' on me, mebbe?' Terpin growled.

'If you want to call it that. I'm here to find out what's causing a lot of Silverdale and Fremont materials to be delayed. I'm here to find out everything I can about whoever is trying to slow up the job, Because I don't know who the opposition really is, I'm going to suspect everybody until I know different. Nothing personal — but that's how it is.'

When none of them had anything to say to that, he added, 'I intended to declare myself to you in a day or so. Evidently your father didn't think I should go unshaved that long.'

Nobody seemed amused at the attempted joke.

'Who have you told about the letter

from your father?' he asked the girl.

'Nobody. That is, only Aunt Hannah.'

The old lady smiled. 'Hannibal and Hannah. Twins. I know that's what you must be thinking.'

Malone returned the smile. It was pleasant to have even a semi-bystander on his side. 'Right. I'm also thinking that it would be a good idea not to spread this around yet. I'd like to look in on the wagon folks this evening, still playing the dirty old mountain man. After that I'll wash my face and you can all get mad at me for sticking my nose into your affairs.'

'I'm sure I'll guard your precious secret carefully,' the girl told him with open irony.

'Thanks. In return I promise you now that I'm not going to interfere in the way anybody's running a job. Matt's supposed to be the best construction boss in the West. I'm not going to tell him how to handle his job. And I think maybe Hannibal knew what he was doing when he sent his daughter out here to look after general operations. I've even got an idea that Flannery is the right man for his chore. I like the way his gang shapes up. I'll ask for help from any of you, but I won't tell you how to handle your business. Is that clear?'

Both Terpin and the girl nodded. They didn't look too enthusiastic.

'So let me tell you what I know,' Malone went on, still trying to ease the situation a little. 'On the train today I saw two men who are notorious troublemakers. I've already told Matt about them, but we've all got to be on the lookout for their tricks. A little fellow named Grimes and a tall thin jigger called Hatfield. Somebody hired 'em. I want to know who did it.'

The girl shook her head. 'I suppose you're right. But I still don't like the way you came up here and tricked us.'

'Sorry,' Malone told her. 'It seemed like the thing to do. My job wasn't set up to make me popular.'

'He's right,' the older woman said quietly. 'I think we'd better get back, Isabel. Give Mr. Malone a chance to show us what he can do.'

'And with no talk — to anybody,' Malone cautioned.

It was the wrong thing to say. Miss Putnam flared again. 'Please give me credit for a little intelligence! I'm quite capable of understanding the importance of this matter!'

★ ★ ★

It was still an hour before dusk when Malone made his way across the drying mud that separated the railroad sidings from the older buildings that the wagoners had set up. Shadows had long since put a chill on the valley, although the sun still touched the snow-clad heights. He moved briskly, partly to keep warm, but remembering that he was not expected to be too spry. This was one time when he would have to remember his role and act it properly. Probably he would have to swallow a lot of things that he would resent. Temper had to be kept strictly under control, and he had purposely

50

come out without any weapons of any kind. A man couldn't learn much by getting involved in a brawl.

He could see that the wagon camp was a bit more substantial than the accompanying settlement by the railroad tracks. With the opening of the mines at Silverdale, it had appeared that the freighters would have a good thing going for them so they had built accordingly. They had not expected a railroad to put them out of business.

Malone looked the place over carefully as he approached it. This could well be the center for the vague threats that had been aimed at the S. & F. There was a good reason why the wagoners would be happy to see their business undisturbed for at least one more season. They knew that their relay town would die as soon as the rail line was completed, so it seemed logical to expect opposition here. The big building Malone had seen from the train looked sturdy, and so did the sheds and corrals. The sign MULESKINNER HOTEL was not as neat as those red and gold affairs that decorated railroad equipment, but the hotel itself seemed pretty substantial. It's owner wouldn't like the idea of abandoning it.

There were few men in sight around the corrals or bunk houses, but that semed natural enough. With the temperature dropping rapidly, the wagon men would be indoors. Smoke spiraling into the sky from a number of buildings suggested that most of them were keeping warm or getting supper — or both.

The big room at the hotel proved to be well filled when Malone went in through heavy log doors that might have been built to stop an Indian raid. A few grimy men, unwashed and unshaven, lounged at the rough bar, but most of the customers were at tables in what seemed to be a big dining room. The bar took up only one end of the place, and it appeared that the Muleskinner Hotel operated something of a restaurant business. Food odors were strong enough to cover the reek of stale beer, spilled whisky, and unwashed bodies. It made Malone remember his earlier impression that this place was a going concern. Whoever was making a good thing of serving food, drinks, and entertainment wouldn't want to have the rug pulled out from under him. The Muleskinner's owner might well be the man behind the threat of trouble.

Malone spotted a long table close to the kitchen door, where Tillie and her girls were seated, accompanied by four men who looked smart enough to know that they would get stuck with the bill. One of them was Jim Hatfield, so Malone moved to a position at the bar where he could keep an eye on the group. Hatfield had always been just a gunman, but on the train he had made that remark about representing the wagon interests. Maybe he would make some move that would show how he was representing them — and who they were.

Not that any serious move on his part seemed likely. All eight of the diners at that particular table were pretty drunk. Tillie seemed to be the soberest of the lot, and she was doing her share of giggling, particularly when a heavy black-bearded teamster leaned across to rub shoulders with her — letting one hairy hand disappear under the table every time he made the move. Hatfield was getting similar giggles from a blond girl who might have been rather pretty if she had not managed to pick up a broken nose at some stage of her career.

The other two men were complete strangers to Malone. Both wore heavy flannel shirts and had leather jackets draped across the backs of their chairs. Malone saw that one of them wore corduroys and high-laced boots like those affected by surveyors. Both were clean-shaven, reasonably young — and ill at ease.

Malone ordered a beer, then stood by the bar nursing it. Careful scrutiny told him nothing. Grimes was not in the room. Except for Hatfield and his party, this was strictly the usual thing, a combination eating-house and saloon catering to pretty rough men.

A narrow-faced man came along

behind the bar and spoke directly to Malone. 'You lookin' to hire on here?' The words were curt, the syllables sharply clipped in an accent that hinted of New England.

Malone turned to stare at the questioner. The little man made him think of that skinny clerk back in the S. & F. office. The two men didn't actually resemble each other, but it was pretty clear that both belonged to what Colorado folks called the One-Lung Army. There was nothing mean-spirited about the term; the tuberculosis patients themselves used it most. To do them justice, many of them were playing a big part in opening up the country they had entered in hopes of prolonging their lives.

'Why should I be hirin' on?' Malone asked, letting his drawl have full sway. 'I jest come around lookin' fer some good grub.' He was getting a good look at the pinched features of the little man. The fellow was probably a tuberculosis victim, well enough, but he was not letting the disease bother him too much.

'Now I see who it is,' the man said with a smile. 'You're the hunter the railroad people sent in. Go ahead over to that table in the corner. We set a real good table here, if I do say it myself.'

'You the boss man around here?' Malone inquired sociably.

'For a while yet. I'm selling out. Going to see if the desert will suit me better than the mountains.'

'But you're still hiring?'

'No. New folks are, though. I just thought I'd ask for them. They hired on a few today.' He grimaced a little as he added, 'Mostly men who came up to work for the railroad. But it's none of my business. If they take up the option, I'll be out of here in a week or so.'

He turned away as though no longer interested in the subject. Malone swallowed the rest of his beer and headed toward the table the little man had indicated. Out of the corner of his eye he saw that Tillie had noticed him. She had pushed away her black-bearded friend and was passing the word to Hatfield.

Malone wondered why. On the train she had seemed only curious, while Hatfield had paid no attention. Now they had enough interest to make both of them turn away from their own individual amusements. He wondered if there could be any connection between that interest and the fact that the saloon proprietor had recieved such prompt information about the S. & F. contract hunter's having arrived on the scene.

A woman of middle age and tremendous hip-breadth brought him what appeared to be the regular supper, not even asking for an order first. He found no reason to complain about the food, either its quality or its quantity, so he gave her the dollar she demanded and went about the business of trying to gauge the meaning of the changed atmosphere at Hatfield's table. Even the broken-nosed blonde seemed to have sobered a little.

It didn't take long for him to decide that he was the subject of the whispers that had taken the place of the giggles.

All the people at the long table shot occasional furtive glances at him, and there were lengthy conferences between Hatfield and Tillie, to the evident discontent of the whiskery muleskinner and the blonde. Malone had to assume that they had found some unusual interest in the fact that the railroad's contract hunter was in camp. He wondered whether something was afoot that a hunter might possibly discover. Perhaps his disgnise had been well chosen.

Grimes came into the room and went directly to Hatfield, pausing to whisper something in the tall man's ear. Hatfield relayed it to Tillie as Grimes went across to sit at a far table and the furtive stares began again. Malone chuckled to himself as he watched it all work out. At least he hadn't made any mistake in thinking that he might stir up a little action by having his supper at the Muleskinner Hotel. So far he had picked up a few ideas — and the action was beginning to show signs of life.

of Jack Kyle.

4

Malone was just finishing his meal when
the conference at the other table seemed
to reach a decision. Tillie's red hair had
been bobbing around vigorously as she
argued with Hatfield, but now her nod
was plain. She was agreeing to something.

It didn't take Jong to see how the decision had gone. The redheaded woman
was getting out of her chair, the green
eyes fixed dubiously on Malone. He had
a feeling that she was still plagued by
a nagging memory, but he didn't think
she would get a real good line on him.
He remembered how he had given her
that leer in the railroad car. That was the
way he would have to play it now. It was
exactly the way Jack Kyle would *not* have
played it. Kyle never talked to people
unless he had to. He generally ignored
dance-hall women, partly because he
couldn't afford to make friends with

59

people who would turn out to be problems in his job. A socially garrulous Malone would never make anyone think of Jack Kyle.

He was planning it all out, rather anticipating the battle of wits, as he saw Hatfield move his chair so that he could keep an eye on things. The Hatfield interest still didn't seem to have much of an explanation. Up to this point, there seemed to be no more than a woman's curiosity involved. Hatfield's evident interest was a trifle ominous. Maybe the situation was more important than it had appeared.

Tillie put on a professional smile as she approached Malone's chair, and he countered by pointing to the vacant chair across the table from him.

'Might as well set yer fanny down, sister,' he greeted in his best drawl. 'I ain't fixin' to git up, so ye might as well keep me from lookin' unpolite. Have a drink?' He was almost proud of the speech. There wasn't a thing in it that remotely sounded like the old Kyle.

She shook her head, red curls flying 'No to both — but thanks. I had plenty to drink and I got a place to sit. I just kinda figured I ought to know you from some place. Before the train, I mean.'

'It ain't likely, ma'am,' Malone told her. 'If'n we'd met before, I reckon I'd remember a purty woman like yerself. And I don't, dagnab it! Yuh sure yuh won't have a drink? We could sorta celebrate almost knowin' each other from some other place and some other time when neither of us was there.'

She laughed at the whimsy but then sobered as much as her condition would permit. 'Are you sure? I keep feeling that I'd know you if you didn't have yourself hid behind those ugly damned whiskers.'

'Well, ma'am, they ain't the purtiest whiskers in the country, I'll admit. But they're the only ones I've got. And I don't reckon the phiz behind 'em would be much purtier.'

Her smile faded. She stared hard once more and then looked around briefly at Hatfield. Malone realized that it was a signal of some sort, but he didn't have any idea what it meant until Tillie backed away from the table with a scream that was as startling as it was artificial.

'I didn't come over here to be insulted!' she yelped. 'Who in hell do you think you are, talkin' like that to a lady?'

Malone didn't bother to reply. Jim Hatfield's prompt move told him that it had been planned this way. Hatfield was storming across the room in carefully feigned indignation. Malone wasn't sure why they should want to involve him in a brawl, but undoubtedly that was the way it was to work.

'What's wrong, Til?' the gunman demanded as he halted unsteadily at the redhead's side.

'This man insulted me! I wouldn't even tell anybody what he suggested.'

Malone thought fast as he got his legs under him. Hatfield usually stayed away from drink when he was on a job, mostly because he couldn't handle his liquor. His putting on an act now hinted that it was something that they had cooked up on the spur of the moment, something that might be turned against the plotters with the right kind of prodding. 'Yuh'd tell anybody anything,' Malone contradicted the woman casually. 'So git off yer high horse. If'n ye're plannin' to stir up a ruckus, let's git it over.'

'Maybe yuh need a lesson in manners, mister,' Hatfield said stiffly. 'Could be I'll give it to yuh right now!'

Malone did some more figuring. Hatfield had his gun under his coat. Even partly drunk, he wouldn't try to use it against an unarmed man. Maybe the prodding campaign was worth a try.

'Ye might git all mussed up,' Malone said sociably. 'Them purty clothes wasn't intended nohow fer brawlin' around with no ole woods cat like me.'

'Woods cat, hell! I know who . . . ' Hatfield broke off abruptly, as though realizing that he had let something slip.

Malone wasn't sure of what the man had almost said, but it seemed like a good time to sound him out as far as possible. The masquerade didn't have long to go, anyway. 'Moral to the story,' he said softly, dropping the drawl. 'Don't play fancy games when you've got a gutful of liquor. You said too much.'

Hatfield bit. 'All right, Mr. Arthur Malone,' he snarled. 'We don't like snoopers any more'n we like . . .'

He was reaching for his gun as he spoke. Maybe he intended to use it as a club, but Malone wasn't taking any chances with a drunken and angry Jim Hatfield. The fellow had too many killings on his record. As the gun came out from beneath the coattails, Malone stepped in, using his left hand to grab the gunman's lean right arm and swinging his right at the man's chin.

Hatfield staggered back but recovered swiftly. There was an instant in which Malone knew that his antagonist was definitely trying to bring the gun into firing position, but he didn't let it happen. Whirling to bring the captured right arm across his own left shoulder, he sent Hatfield flying through the air, the gun skidding across the floor under the table.

The crash of the gunman's fall brought a flat silence to the room, and Malone seized the opportunity to announce calmly, 'Get on with your eating, folks. Fight's over.'

A shout from the direction of the bar told him that he had made the same mistake that Hatfield had made, over-playing his hand. The little proprietor was coming out from behind the bar, a shotgun leveled at the prostrate Hatfield.

'Drop it!' the little man barked. 'Any shootin' around here I'm doin'!'

Hatfield let a hideout gun slip from his fingers. He climbed awkwardly to his feet, staggered back to the big table as the shotgun waved him along. The little man waited until the gunnie was back with his companions, then went over to pick up both weapons.

'Everybody understand this!' he announced loudly. 'Brian Guinn's still boss here. No shootin' is the rule, like always. I'll let you all know when anybody else starts runnin' this place.'

He turned to look at Malone. 'Done with your supper?' he asked.

'Almost.'

'Then get done. I don't know what this was all about, but I don't have no brawlin' around here.'

'Suits me,' Malone said. 'You're Guinn?'

'That's right.'

'Good. I'm Lefty Malone. You didn't seem to know, but Hatfield did, that I'm taking charge of construction for the S. & F. We might as well understand each other.'

The little man stared. 'In that outfit?' He grinned crookedly. 'I guess I understand. You wanted to know what Hatfield's crowd is aiming to do.'

'Something like that. Anything you want to tell me — while we're so sociable?'

'No. Because I don't know a thing about it. I gave Hatfield an option on what I own here. I was aiming to sell out anyway just as soon as the rail line went through. Heading for Arizona.'

'Hatfield has the option?'

'Right.'

'Who else?'

'I don't know. My deal was with him. Nobody else was mentioned.' He started to turn away, but then added, 'You'd be smart to get out of here when you're done with your eatin'. I don't like the look o' those two varmints who've been hanging around waiting for Hatfield to show up.'

He moved away quickly, keeping an angry eye on the long table. Malone found himself grinning appreciatively at the little man's back. Brian Guinn might be an invalid, but he had guts. And he had undoubtedly saved Malone's life. Hatfield on the floor with a hideout gun would have been as deadly as a rattlesnake. Not many men had ever knocked Jim Hatfield down and lived to tell about it.

Malone knew that this would not be the end of the affair, but he didn't let his mind dwell on it. Two important points had just presented themselves. Guinn was selling — but had not yet sold — to a company that seemed to be using Hatfield as its front man. That could explain a lot of things. The other point wasn't so openly significant, but Malone had a hunch that it might prove to be worth attention. The two furtive strangers had been at Muleskinner for some time, waiting for Hatfield to arrive. There had to be a connection.

It was easy to concentrate now, Malone discovered. He no longer had to play the role he had been trying. That was a help. It also had another advantage — or so he hoped. Now that he had let people see a personality behind the character he had first appeared to be, it seemed likely that they would not suspect that still another identity was concealed. Only Hannibal Putnam knew the truth. Malone did'nt propose to share the confidence with anyone else.

He was about ready to stop dallying with his food, feeling that he had stuck around long enough to let people know that he was not being scared off, when he saw that something was developing at the big table. He sat back and made a slow job of his last sips of coffee.

At first the moves were being made by the women. Tillie announced loudly that her girls would be back for the usual evening's entertainment, and the four of them swept out of the place, only the blonde staggering enough to be conspicuous. Then Hatfield and the other men went into a quick huddle that broke up in a matter of seconds. The two men Guinn had mentioned slid out of their chairs and went out, speaking to no one on the way to the door.

Moments later, Hatfield crossed to the bar and claimed his guns from Guinn, getting them after a little delay. He also went out into the darkness. The black-bearded man didn't move until Malone pushed back his chair and started toward the bar. Then the fellow went across the room to take a seat in the corner with Carl Grimes. Somehow the moves all seemed to be part of a neat little program.

Malone knew that he was in trouble.

He didn't have a gun, and he had a lot of open space to cross before he could get back to the railroad town. As soon as he left the table, he saw Blackbeard get up and head for the door. That did it, Hatfield was being warned that his victim was on his way.

There was just time for Malone to catch Brian Guinn's eye as the whiskery man went out. 'Don't stop me,' Malone said shortly, 'I'm going back through the kitchen. I think you know why.'

He registered the little man's nod and was on his way, changing direction and heading for the kitchen door. Apparently no one paid any attention. In the kitchen, he ignored the stout woman's challenge and hurried between tables, keeping out of reach of the cleaver that the Chinese cook was waving at him. Only a few strides and be was under the stars behind the building, where he paused brielly so that his eyes could adjust to the darkness.

The mud was beginning to have the suspicion of a crust on it from the temperature's nightly drop, but he could move on it without making much noise. A cautious glance around the east corner of the big rambling hotel revealed a man standing in the shadows near the front of the place. He tried the other end, first having to grope his way past stacks of empty boxes and crates. When be peered around the west corner, he saw another, deeper shadow in the gloom. He guessed that Hatfield had posted the two strangers as guards, Probably they were waiting for Malone to come out the front door. Then there would be a man on either side of him to make sure that he didn't get away before Hatfield could avenge the indignity that had been heaped upon him.

Malone wasted a moment on wondering whether this was just another Hatfield show of viciousness or whether the gunman wanted to get rid of a man who was known to represent the railroad company. It didn't seem worthwhile to make guesses now. Before long, the men out front would learn that their intended victim had left by a back door. Malone didn't propose to go unarmed against Hatfield and his gang, particularly in a chase in which he would be the hunted,

Since he didn't know where Hatfield and the black-bearded man had located themselves, he made his move on little more than a hunch. His idea was to get rid of one of the guards as quickly as possible, and he picked the one on the east, reasoning that sunlight would have warmed the ground enough on that side so that there wouldn't be enough ice crust to betray his movements. The west had been in shadow even before the sun went behind the mountains, so it figured to be a riskier side for silent movement.

He moved slowly, making certain to avoid any loose trash and the worst of the mud. In a few seconds he could make out the outline of the guard, a bit of light from the front windows of the Muleskinner serving to silhouette the man. It was one of the pair that had come into the mountains ahead of Hatfield, and the man was peering around the front corner of the hotel, his gun in his hand.

Malone hit him in the back of the neck with a hard fist, and the man went down without even a grunt. It took a moment to haul him back into the shadows, and by that time Malone had his gun and the man was beginning to grunt. So Malone hit him over the head with the gun. It was not a moment too soon. Heels were rattling along the brief stretch of plank walkway in front of the hotel.

Hatfield's voice came cautiously but with a note of emergency in it. 'Come on outa there, Tucker! The bastard went out the back way. Walt and Blackie are tryin' to head him off on the far side.'

Malone growled something, testing the gun in his fingers. He saw the tall shadow of Hatfield coming toward him, the gunman too anxious to be properly cautious. He was snapping his orders in a guarded tone as he reached the corner of the building — and then Malone let him have it, swinging the captured gun hard against the side of Hatfield's skull. This time he didn't need a second blow to dispose of his man.

While dragging his second victim into the shadows, he came up with an idea. He placed Hatfield carefully beside the man who had been hailed as Tucker. Then he put the gun into Tucker's limp hand and calmly walked away. He had a small regret that he couldn't be around when the pair woke up and began to curse each other. Maybe it would get even better. Maybe Walt or Blackie would find them like that before they came to their senses. One way or another, it would be an interesting scene.

Terpin was sitting on his bunk in the warehouse when Malone went in, only the glow of his stogie marking his presence. He wasted no time in making his challenge, his voice so low that he didn't sound like the same man.

'Kinda chummy with Brian Guinn, I hear,' he greeted. 'Seems like a mighty odd way fer a man to act when he's supposed to be lookin' out fer Quinn's kind o' troublemakin'.'

'News travels fast,' Malone retorted. 'Almost as fast in one direction as in the other. How much did you hear?'

'Enough. Ye got into a fight with a feller at the Muleskinner, and Guinn bailed yuh out of it. How come yuh're so friendly with him?'

'I'll answer your question if you'll answer mine first. How many people did you tell that I'm Old Pot's partner?'

'Not a damned one. Why?'

'Because Hatfield knew. Guinn didn't.'

'That don't make sense. There wasn't much time fer anybody to find out. Yuh think mebbe this here Hatfield knowed about yuh before he arrived?'

'No. His actions on the train weren't those of a man who knew such a thing.'

'Now yuh're guessin'.'

'Maybe. But I'd bet on it. Somebody got the word to Hatfield during the hour after I talked to you and the Putnam women. I think we'd better take steps to find out who it was.' He went on to tell Terpin of the events at the Muleskinner. He wasn't too sure why he trusted a man like Matt Terpin, but he had a feeling that for once in his crooked career

Terpin was playing a straight game. Better to risk telling him everything and hope that he was going to turn out all right There was one thing to be considered: if Terpin was working against the S. & F., there wasn't much chance of stopping the trouble. Better to trust the fat man all the way.

Terpin chuckled happily at the description of how Hatfield and Tucker had been left, but then he rumbled, 'It ain't good. That wagon outfit's the one we got to watch. Nobody else has got so much reason to want to stop us. If Guinn's sellin' out, like he claims, we got to find out who's buyin'. Better have Miss Isabel git word to her old man.',

'Not yet. Maybe she's the one let the word get out.'

'Not Miss Isabel, mister. She's all right.'

'Get some sleep,' Malone advised. 'Maybe we'll smoke out the wrong one in the morning. If we've got a traitor on the payroll, we've got to find out who it is.'

76

5

When Malone opened his eyes next morning, it was full daylight and Terpin was gone. He lay under his blankets for a couple of minutes, not quite ready to climb out into the chill, and reviewed anew the facts he had learned earlier. A new day didn't change his opinion very much. The railroad had enemies who were trying to stop or delay construction. As yet there was no hint as to who those enemies were, but it seemed pretty certain that they had taken pains to remain in the background. The hiring of Hatfield as a front and the option bought from Brian Guinn suggested money. It was still too soon to guess where Grimes fitted in. Malone didn't think that the man would stop at simply spreading rumors about Indian threats.

He finally rolled out when he heard singing. There was a single window in the front of the building, so he went across to it and stared out at the gang

of men who were hitching up several of
the new grading carts. Flannery's gang
was wasting no time. The graders would
be in the proper places as soon as the
ground thawed. Meanwhile they were
sounding off with their own version of
Finnegan's Wake.

Old Flannery's boss of a handsome
  crew,
A passel o' gintlemen one and all.
His beautiful brogue is rich and
  sweet.
It's music enough when he starts to
  bawt
No matter he's fond of his tipplin'
  ways,
For the love o' hard licker old Denny
  was born.
When he's drunk we shove him
  right outa the way;
He'll drink straight through from
  the break of morn.

Wid me philalloo, hubbaboo, whack
  hurroo, boys,

Didn't we sing 'til our jaws did ache,
And shout and laugh and drink and
    sing,
Oh, it's lots o' fun at Flannery's
    wake.

'Noisy bastards,' Terpin observed, easing himself through the doorway, which was none too wide for his bulk. 'They work like hell with it, so I ain't complainin'.'

'What about Flannery? He like it?'

'Sure. He ain't a drinkin' man, so his gang has got their selves a whole passel o' verses about him bein' drunk. While they're havin' a joke at him, they keep workin'. That's our aim.'

'That's the way I figured it was. And don't think I'm complaining. Like I told you last night, I'm not up here to poke my nose into your job or anybody else's. The big idea is that I'm going to try like hell lo see to it that you have a chance to get the job done. You and everybody else.'

'What was yuh plannin' to do about

that business o' somebody leakin' news to the enemy camp?'

'I'm not sure. I can't prove anything — and the news that went across wasn't important. Word would be out today anyhow. Maybe we'll play stupid a bit and see who makes the next move.'

Terpin grinned. 'Sneaky, hey? I kinda like that.' Then he added, 'Better git over to the cook shack if'n yuh want any breakfast. The greasy pot gang is as ornery as the rest o' the crew. They don't give a damn fer bosses.'

Malone smiled. 'Right away. I'm beginning to think you've got yourself quite an outfit up here. These ornery types generally work good.'

'Want me fer anything?' the fat man asked. 'I'm goin up the grade and have a look at how Flannery's fixin' to beat the thaw.' His tone hinted that he had decided to recognize Malone's authority.

'I told you before, Matt, that I'm not here to give you orders. It's your job; handle it your own way. One thing, though — it might be a good idea if you went along with me when I look in at the office. When I throw out some hints about leaks, it would be a help if there were two of us to watch for reactions.'

Terpin grinned. 'Sneaky, hey? Mebbe you and me is goin' to git along real good . . . Lefty.'

'Let's make it about two hours from now. 'That'll suit you, won't it?'

'How'd yuh know?'

'The train should be coming up about then. You want to see how many new men Old Put sent, don't you?'

The fat man grinned again. 'Seems like we understand each other. See yuh later.'

Malone managed to get some breakfast with no more than a tirade from the cross-eyed cook, who was almost as fat as Matt Terpin. The man cursed contract hunters in general and late-rising ones in particular — but he set out a good meal. Malone enjoyed the food as much as he appreciated the evidence that the cook didn't know that he was cursing a new boss. Obviously Terpin had not let the secret get to the men.

It was easy to carry the reasoning a little further. Hatfield's hasty words had not been meaningful to anyone else, so the truth would not have gotten out from anything that had happened at the Muleskinner Saloon. Since there had clearly been no gossip about it at the cook shack, it was certain that Terpin had not done any talking to other men in the crew. Unless the fat man had sent word directly to Hatfield — which Malone doubted very much — then the leak was connected with Isabel Putnam. That part of it Malone didn't like at all.

As soon as he had eaten, he went back to the warehouse and proceeded to change his appearance. Shaving off the whiskers was something of a chore, but he managed it, using a small mirror that hung over Terpin's bunk. The result satisfied him. There was no more of Jack Kyle in the smoothly shaven, angular face than there had been in the bewhiskered one. Many times during the past three years he had recalled the elaborate pretense that had been so much a part of the Kyle personality. Usually it was embarrassing to him when he remembered what a thorough fake he had been, but now he could take some satisfaction in it. That carefully dyed mustache and goatee combination had been asinine enough, but they had identified Kyle. A smooth face would remind no one of the man who no longer existed.

A flannel shirt from his war bag took the place of the buckskin garment, although he stuck with the same old breeches, having nothing at hand to replace them with. Company stores would take care of that matter later. Now he was only interested in making a change in his appearance that would be identified with his new role. Making it all very simple might keep people from doing too much thinking.

He set off to make the rounds of the supply area, checking on the materials at hand and studying the way they had been set up for easy access against the time when the work crews would need them. Once more he could feel satisfaction at what he was seeing. Everything was organized well. The rails would be pushed out rapidly if outside trouble could be prevented.

He was still studying and appraising when the distant scream of a train whistle interrupted his thoughts. He smiled at the sound. Somehow those little three-foot-gauge teakettles always were equipped with whistles that sounded childish. Maybe a man who had helped build full-size railroads tended to be a little scornful of the narrow lines. And that wasn't very smart. Narrow gauge saved a lot of work in this mountain country.

He headed back toward the office just in time to meet Terpin. The fat man waved a big hand back toward the area where Flannery's men were starting to bite into the grade that would take the line up into Muleskinner Gulch. 'Doin' real good up there,' he reported. 'We kin use a full crew in another three-four days if the weather stays good. Goin' to drop in at the office before the train comes in?'

'Seems like a good idea. A quick visit ought to do the trick. Then we meet the train and watch for the pot to boil.'

Terpin grinned his appreciation. Today his voice was under control, and Malone wondered whether the fact had any significance that he hadn't caught. It was hard to remember that he had decided to trust Matt Terpin.

They found the office much as it had been on the previous day. No new men were being signed on — since none had yet arrived — but the clerks were busy. Wheeler had another big stack of papers in front of him, and he didn't even look up when the two men entered.

Isabel Putnam stared for a moment and then smiled. 'I didn't know you,' she told Malone frankly. 'You look a lot younger without those horrible whiskers.'

He nodded but did not smile. 'Thanks. But I didn't come around to exchange compliments. I discovered last evening that my identity was already known over at the Muleskinner Hotel. I've checked pretty thoroughly, and I don't believe that Matt spilled the beans. Now, I'd like to know who might have gotten the information from you.' He was purposely making himself sound pretty stiff.

Miss Putnam flushed angrily, much as he had expected her to do. 'If you are suggesting that I said anything to anybody you are entirely mistaken! And I resent the suggestion!'

'I believe you — and I apologize. Now tell me this. Who could have seen your father's letter?'

'No one.'

'Are you sure? Where was it when you came to the warehouse to accuse me of being myself?'

'Why . . . ' She hesitated, some of the anger turning to doubt. 'It was right here in my desk.'

'I had a hunch it was that way. Who could have poked around and found it?' He had taken a position from which he could watch the reactions of both Wheeler and Withers.

There was a nervous little movement

from the clerk, but then Wheeler stood up at his desk. 'I'm sure I don't know what this is all about, but I am hearing enough to make me understand that something is amiss. Let me assure you that no one went near Miss Putnam's desk while she was away from the office!'

'Thanks,' Malone said dryly. 'And let me fill you in. I'm Lefty Malone, Hannibal Putnam's partner. Miss Putnam can supply the details and tell you about me later. We'll follow up this matter after we see who's coming in on the train. Come along, Matt. Let's find out if you've got any workmen on the train.'

No other word was spoken until Malone and Terpin were moving down the track toward the spot where the coach would stop. Then the fat man wheezed, 'How come yuh broke it off so sharp in there? I thought yuh was goin' to see if somebody would crack under a bit o' proddin'.'

'No need,' Malone told him. 'Wheeler's the sour apple in our barrel.'

'Jest because he talked sharp?'

'No. When I sprung my question about the desk, I got a fast move from Withers. The little jigger was itching to say something, but Wheeler got his two cents' worth in first.'

'Ain't that kind of imaginin' things?' Terpin was laboring to keep his voice down. It seemed almost painful for him to do it.

'Think about it,' Malone invited. 'If the clerk had been messing around Miss Putnam's desk, Wheeler would have told us about it in a hurry. But Wheeler's kind of a boss over Withers. When he claimed that neither of them was at the desk, Withers couldn't make up his mind to contradict him.'

'That's where I come in,' Terpin growled. 'I'll git the truth out of him!'

'Don't bother. Let's give Wheeler a chance to show his hand. It might be better if he thinks we're fooled. And he'd find out for sure if you strong-armed that little varmint. I don't think Withers is the same kind of a one-lunger that Brian Guinn is. He wouldn't hold up.'

They watched the work train arrive with its supplies and its one forlorn little passenger coach. Today Malone could notice that the car, which Putnam had bought from another narrow-gauge line, was badly in need of paint, only the bright lettering above its windows appeared fresh and new. He made a mental note to tell Hannibal that he ought to get enough paint for the whole car. Then he found something better to think about. Carl Grimes was hurrying across to where the train was just sliding to a halt.

'Looks like Grimes is a little late getting over to try his scare talk,' he commented to Terpin. 'I wonder if he had anybody on the car to do his talking today?'

'That's Grimes, hey?' the fat man growled. 'Yuh goin' to let him mess around?'

'No. You get ready to see that your men move right along to the hiring office. I think it's time I put a bug in the Grimes ear.'

He intercepted the little man just as

89

the train ground to a halt. 'You're in the wrong place, Mr. Grimes,' he said, loudly enough to be heard above the roar of the little engine. 'Turn right around and head back to the wagon town. Now!'

The way he barked the final word took something out of the little man. Grimes hesitated but then tried to argue. 'This is public, mister. I got a right to . . .'

Malone didn't wait to hear any of the famous Grimes argument. 'You've got no right to do anything here. Until this railroad line is open for business, it's private property — even if you rode on the train yesterday. But we won't worry the point. The big thing is that I'm kinda running things here — and I don't want you hanging around.'

When Grimes tried to say something, Malone moved a step closer. 'It happens that I remember a gent up at Shoshone Bend. He got killed in a riot that you started, you sneaky little bastard. Don't make me remember things like that or maybe I'll do more than this.' He reached out with one hand to slap the derby hat

to do.

'Let him go,' Malone advised finally. 'I guess these men have heard enough so they'll understand that a gang of crooks are trying to keep us from building this railroad.

'Maybe they won't listen to the next cock-and-bull story the opposition dreams up.' He was moderately pleased that the morning had worked out as it had. Getting a confession from even such a poor stick as this toothless character was a help. Word would get around. Some of the men who had gone over to the wagon camp would hear about it and come back. Word should be sent out to Hannibal Putnam. Maybe it would help him with his hiring problems.

The toothless man finally persuaded Terpin to accept him as a hostler for the S. & F. Apparently he was not too happy at the way his employment with Grimes had worked out.

There was plenty of amused talk about it at the hiring end of the office building when Malone went in to speak again with Miss Putnam. He told her what he knew about both Grimes and Hatfield, announcing, 'I think we've licked them on this business of trying to keep us from getting full crews. Now we'll have to see what they do next.' He made no mention of his certainty that someone in the S. & F. office was supplying information to the enemy.

'Can you prove any of this about Grimes being a hired trouble-maker?' Miss Putnam asked when he'd sketched in the man's history in other sore spots.

'Why prove it? We're not trying to prosecute him in court. I know it's true. We know he's up to his old tricks here. That's enough. We look out for him.'

'And Hatfield?'

'We keep an eye on him, too. My guess is that he makes the next real move, now that we've got Grimes stopped.'

He went out to talk briefly with Terpin about the assignment of the new men. Twenty of them were to be sent on into the gulch on the following morning, to be ready when O'Boyle could begin operations at the other camp. The rest would be assigned to Flannery — except for a pair who would drive the wagon with its blasting powder. Terpin had already picked the men for that chore. The toothless new hostler was to go as driver. Accompanying him as a shotgun guard would go a quarrelsome character who was causing a bit of trouble on Flannery's gang.

'He don't fit with Flannery's ornery crowd. They're a bunch o' noisy apes, but they don't need somebody standin over 'em with a pick handle all the time. This here polecat will work better when Shawn O'Boyle is callin' the turns.'

'That's what you're here for,' Malone told him. 'To decide things like that. I'll try to make sure that you have a free hand — mostly by keeping the opposition under control.'

He felt that he was accomplishing a part of his job when he saw Carl Grimes hurry across the drying mud and jump aboard the train as it started to back down the grade that afternoon. He couldn't be

95

sure whether the little man had made his own decision to get out or whether word had gone over from the S. & F. office that Grimes was no longer useful. Wheeler had made a trip to the corrals soon after Malone's visit to the office. Minutes later a railroad hostler named Leon had hurried across to the Muleskinner Hotel. Malone had to argue Terpin out of beating the truth out of the hostler.

'I think we've got our leak spotted now. Let's leave it that way. The next move is likely lo be a rough one — with Hatfield calling the shots. We'd better have one small advantage, even if it's nothing but a knowledge of traitors in our own camp.'

'Jest one thing,' Terpin growled. 'When the time comes — let me take a crack at 'em.'

'Don't be anxious,' Malone advised dryly. 'With Hatfield on the job — and plenty sore — we may be pretty busy defending ourselves.'

6

There was a message from Isabel Putnam shortly after noon. She had digested a letter from her father and wanted to pass along the information in it. He was still having difficulty in getting men to sign up for work in country where there was supposed to be danger of Indian trouble. Several carloads of rails had been diverted over the Denver and Rio Grande and had turned up in Pueblo instead of at Fremont Junction. Nobody could find out how the wrong orders had been issued, but it seemed pretty certain that this was another of the calculated attempts to delay S. & F. construction. In this case it hadn't hurt. There were plenty of rails on hand. Such a trick later in the summer when supplies needed to flow freely would be a different story.

The other item of interest was that Brian Guinn's story had been confirmed. Guinn's wagon outfit had been optioned by a company known as the Rocky Mountain Freighters. The only man listed as having anything to do with company administration was one James Hatfield. Putnam didn't seem to think that it was important.

Malone accepted the information without comment. Only when he was leaving the office did he say, 'Better take the letter to your quarters with you, Miss Putnam. It doesn't seem safe to leave that kind of thing in your desk.' He wasn't ready to call Wheeler to account, but it seemed like a good idea to keep the man a little nervous.

Back at the warehouse he prepared for his trip into the mountains with Terpin and then wrote out a lengthy report to Hannibal Putnam. After that he wandered casually along to the rooms that served as quarters for Isabel Putnam and her aunt.

His timing was good. There was just time for him to exchange a couple of banal remarks with the old lady before Isabel came in. Her greeting was cool enough to make it clear that she didn't approve of him.

'I'm surprised, Mr. Malone. A little while ago you didn't seem to be interested in anything that I might have to say.'

'Sorry if it seemed that way. I didn't want to talk in front of Wheeler.'

Her frown deepened. 'Don't tell me you're seriously charging him with being a traitor?'

'That's exactly the case. I'm not charging him because I can't prove it — and maybe we'll do better to let him think that he's not suspected but . . .'

'You don't need to say any more. It seems to me that you're borrowing a great deal of trouble. So far we've had no serious problems except a lot of senseless gossip about Indians. I can't get very excited because a couple of your old friends happen to turn up at the wagon camp.'

He shrugged. It was no time to get involved in an argument. 'I'm afraid I'll have to ask you to play it my way. Don't leave anything confidential in your desk. And we'll discuss nothing of importance in the office.'

'Now you sound like the boss.' There was plenty of ice in her tone.

'That's why I'm here. At the camp, I mean. The reason I'm here in this room is that I've got a letter I want you to send out to your father — without Wheeler knowing about it. Read it. It'll be easier for you to get the facts that way than by listening and interrupting while I tell you.'

She met his glance grimly. 'You do manage to be nasty, don't you?'

'Just blunt. You'll note that I've explained why I don't believe that Jim Hatfield is anything but a straw boss. Maybe your father can find out who hired him and why. Until we know about that part, we've got to be on the lookout for anything.'

'Very dramatic!' she mocked.

'Read the letter,' he repeated. 'And trust Flannery if you run into trouble. I'm going up to the other camp with

Matt in the morning. I don't know when I'll be back.'

'I'll do my best to get along without you,' she told him.

He grinned. 'You sure got a dose of the old man's vinegar in you. Too bad you didn't inherit a bit of his good sense.' He headed for the door, grim but a little pleased to see the smile that the old lady was aiming at him. Then he tried to forget the whole thing. He had to get on with the business of letting Matt Terpin build a railroad.

After supper, at the company's cook shack, he learned that Terpin had made his arrangements for the following morning. The two men he had picked for the job were to start out with the wagonload of blasting powder a full hour before daylight They had their orders, but no one else was to know when the powder would be moved. At dawn twenty men for O'Boyle's gang would move out with ten of the new grading carts. Their departure would get plenty of attention, just in case anybody was watching.

'You and me will ride the survey line,' he told Malone. 'It's all brushed out fer the graders so we won't be havin' no hard ridin'. And it'll save us wallerin' through the mud in the gulch bottom.'

That was the way it worked. Terpin and Malone headed up the line that Flannery's gang had started to grade, their course roughly parallel to the one the new men were taking with the tilt-up carts. Malone had already sized up the situation on his earlier trip out to the end of grade. The wagon outfits had been using Muleskinner Gulch to the point where the steep climb into the pass had required the extra teams. To avoid that impossible grade, the rail road had to climb a little more gradually. The rails would follow the sides of Muleskinner Gulch instead of the bottom, gaining height so that a wide circle around a couple of peaks would permit an easy entrance into the pass. A train would cover several miles more than the wagon route, but that was the way it had to be.

'One thing I didn't tell yuh,' Terpin remarked as they eased along the slope where they could look back down into the gulch at the first of the tip-ups on the wagon trail 'We had a couple o' fires. Tie piles. That's when they started talkin' about the Utes bein' out to bust us up. Yuh figger we might have any trouble with Injuns?'

'Nobody ever knows about Indians. But I'm betting against it. Who seemed to do the talking?'

'Hard to tell where it got started. Main idea was that our loop to the east will run across the shoulder of a mountain that the redskins think is Manitou country. I ain't even sure which mountain it is.'

Malone didn't want to rule out any possibilities. A lot of people had gotten themselves killed because white men didn't pay much attention to the way the Sioux considered the Black Hills as some kind of holy ground. Still, it seemed funny that there had never been any talk about this part of the mountains being sacred among the Utes until the rail line was planned. And there had been no Indian objections when the surveying parties did their work on the mountain in question.

'Part of a campaign,' he said finally. 'Scare workmen away. Burn supplies. Mix-ups in our shipments. None of it amounts to much, but all of it put together could mean a lot of delay. And we can't afford delay. This line has to be running not much later than midsummer or we're all in a mess.'

'That's what keeps me thinkin' about them wagon folks,' Terpin said. 'They're the ones stand to gain by holdin' us up. They must know that they can't keep the line from gittin' finished, but it'll mean a lot o' dollars to 'em if'n it don't git done this year. Who else stands to gain?'

'That's what we've got to find out.'

They moved rapidly until they reached a spot where they could see a six-mule team ahead of them. It was the powder wagon, and Terpin sighed in gusty relief at sight of it.

'Doin' all right,' he declared. 'Looks

like mebbe we didn't let the beans git spilled this time. Ain't no sign o' anybody botherin' around.'

Malone was willing to join in the feeling of satisfaction. This was the kind of morning when a man didn't want to find trouble. The air still had the crispness that came from the snows around them, but the sun was bright and mountain flowers were beginning to put a twinkle of color into the very edges of the melting snow patches.

They rode above the laboring powder wagon for another half mile, but then Terpin proposed that they cut through the timber and save a little distance. 'Rails have got to climb along the top of a cliff up ahead but then they swing into the first big hook. We'll hit it easier by goin' across the near side o' the mountain.'

It put them on the south slope of the rise, where there was no snow to hinder progress. Good game country, Malone thought. Too bad he couldn't have played the role of hunter for a while. It would have been a lot more fun than fighting an enemy who refused to show himself except through the agency of hired thugs like Hatfield.

Not that Hatfield wasn't bad enough. The man was dangerous at any time, and now he would be deadlier than usual. Malone let a wry smile tug at the newly shaven lip as he wondered how well the enemy had figured out the recent combat. Probably they knew that the bewhiskered man who had thrown Hatfield across the saloon was the same clean-shaven fellow who had ordered Grimes away from railroad property. But had they figured out the part about Hatfield and Tucker being laid out so cozily together? Perhaps there had even been some violent misunderstanding between them over the matter; at least none of them had appeared since that evening. And perhaps that was one reason why Grimes had left the valley so promptly. Perhaps he had to get back to headquarters and report trouble among the front-line troops.

He told Terpin what he was thinking,

but the fat man shook his head. 'Boys seen Grimes talkin' to Hatfield jest before the little bastard jumped the down train. And Tucker was eatin' with Hatfield at noon yestiday.'

Malone looked around curiously. 'Seems like you have a few spies of your own on the job.'

The fat man winked happily. 'I'm as sneaky as the next feller. Now that we know who's against us, we'll keep right good track o' their doin's.'

They halted a few minutes later where a shoulder of the mountain made a ridge that stuck almost straight into the north. 'This is where we git the rails up to a spot what'll let us git over the pass,' Terpin explained. 'Yuh kin see the survey line ahead. We're near two miles high right now. Rail summit ain't quite that much.' He pointed out the way the track would work across the side of the ridge to hit the gap the wagons now used after their double-team climb. Malone knew by this time that Terpin was as good a man at his job as his reputation said he was. He thoroughly understood the job in front of him, and he knew every foot of the line that he was supposed to put down. For a man of no education, he understood the engineering problems astonishingly well.

'We kin edge into the pass from here,' he told Malone, 'or we could ease back there and make sure that our blastin' powder's gettin' up the grade. With so much mud, it could be we'll have to throw our ropes on the wagon and give the mules a bit of help.'

Malone was curious to see the famous grade out of Muleskinner Gulch, so he nodded and the two of them swung on around the mountain. Terpin began to explain again, pointing out a part of the survey line that they had not seen in their circling of the mountain. 'Kind of a tricky bit fer more'n a mile. Line's goin' to run right along the top of a rock cliff. Best part is that we don't need to do much blastin'. Heavy charges might knock the whole damned thing down and then we'd have to cut back into the mountain. By usin' the cliff it oughta save us two three weeks.'

They were moving into the hard-climbing stretch where the cliff top towered over the sloping canyon floor when Malone pointed to a double set of tracks in a patch of snow where the pines had held back the sun's thawing effect. 'Two riders. Not long ago. Any of your men supposed to be up here?'

Terpin hesitated. 'Might be O'Boyle's got hunters out.' He grinned crookedly as he explained, 'That huntin' idea ain't a bad one. O'Boyle's been doin' it ever since he took men out to the upper camp. Kinda like givin' 'em time off — and it helps the meat supply a hell of a lot.'

Malone knew that the fat man was laughing at him for the way he had argued the point in favor of having a hunter supply meat to the upper camp. 'So you boys were ahead of us,' he said shortly. 'Right now I want to know about these tracks. I think they were made not more than an hour or so ago. What about miners, prospectors, or somebody

109

like that? Who's living in this part of the country?'

'Nobody. Not even the Utes they talk about.'

'We won't worry about Utes. These were shod ponies Let's see where they were going.'

That part was simple enough. The two riders had followed the railroad's survey line, heading back toward Muleskinner along the top of the cliff the fat man had been discussing Malone could see the point in the construction plans now. At some points the cliff top was a mere shelf on the mountain, a shelf that might not accommodate a full-size rail road. The three-foot gauge could use it, but there wouldn't be much room to spare.

Terpin seemed to sense trouble. He urged his horse forward as they picked up the trail of the unknown riders. Over his shoulder he explained loudly, 'Ain't no reason fer nobody to hit the trail at that point. Nobody woulda been comin' in from the east. None o' Shawn's boys would ride this way if they was headin' fer Muleskinner. Looks to me like somebody was takin' a fast look at this part of the line — likely fer a bit o' hell.'

Malone didn't need to have that explained. This stretch was a weak point in the S. & F. defenses. Interference with construction at this point might prove to be very costly. Terpin was right in wanting to know who might be examining the possibilities.

They crossed the level part of the cliff top at a fast pace, but then Terpin yelled and pointed to where the hoof tracks began to angle down the step-like side of the mountain beyond the cliff's end. 'Them polecats went right down to the wagon track from here. Yuh think it was less'n an hour ago?'

'About an hour. Hard to tell. What's below here?'

'Jest mud. This is where the wagon trail starts goin' down-grade past the cliff and then has to climb back up to the pass. Them bastards coulda been along here just about the right time to meet our blastin' powder.'

'Why?'

'I dunno. That's what worries me, the things I can't figger out.'

He set his weary horse to the down slope, riding hard through brush as they dropped away from the survey line. There was no snow on this slope, but the tracks were clear enough. Clear enough for Malone to think that perhaps he had made a mistake. These tracks were older than he had guessed. In places — the spots where morning sun would have thawed the ground late — they were scarcely visible.

'They're more than an hour ahead of us,' he yelled to the hurrying Terpin. 'No use tryin' to catch them now.'

The trail the fat man now followed was a twisting path down into the narrow gulch, and it was slightly amazing to Malone that anyone as bulky as Matt Terpin could handle a horse on such a grade — or that the horse could keep his feet. Now he pulled up, pointing back toward the cliff from whose top they were descending. 'I ain't hurryin' to ketch 'em,' he explained. 'But we might need to bust in on what they're doin'. I been thinkin' about what would happen if somebody would blow up a load o' blastin' powder there at the bottom o' the cliff. Two bastards circlin' around here jest ahead of a powder wagon don't add up to no happy games.'

Malone had seen enough to understand. A well-placed blast could bring the cliff down, leaving no place for the railroad track — and blocking the temporary supply line to the camp and the mines. He could understand Terpin's alarm. He shared it. 'Get moving,' he said shortly.

They had to swing out along one of the ledges that made up this part of the slope, and far below them they could see the six-mule team laboring up the grade toward them. Malone estimated that one of the high points in the wagon trail was almost directly below his present position. From this point it would be downhill for the wagons until they partly passed the long cliff. Then they had to start the big climb to the pass. Apparently the two riders they were now trailing had studied the country enough to realize that this was the best place for an ambush of a wagon. At least that was the way it looked.

'They're doin' all right so far,' Terpin shouted. 'Danger point's right below us.'

'Any way to get down quick without bein seen?'

'Nope. Them bastards ahead of us seemed to know how to do it. We better keep follerin' 'em 'til we know fer sure what kind o' hell they're up to.' He was kneeing his horse into the downgrade once more as he yelled the words. That was one good thing about riding with Terpin, Malone thought whimsically; a man could always depend on hearing him. He hoped the potential enemy wouldn't.

They brushed through small pines on the sloping mountainside, always dropping lower but now unable to see anything of the gulch trail. Malone calculated that the powder wagon must be directly below them now and not too far away. Still there had been no sign of the trouble he had been anticipating. Maybe a man let his imagination run away with him at a time like this.

The trail swung out to another ledge, and they could see down into the gulch once more. Below them and about two hundred yards to the left, the powder wagon was rolling along, the two men on its seat evidently drunk enough to be pretty hilarious. They were singing loudly, one of them interrupting the other and making him repeat. Malone got the idea. The older employee was teaching the new one some of the home-made verses of *Flannery's Wake*.

'Bastards!' Terpin roared. 'I told that goddam Beals to stay sober. He ain't even got his rifle ready — and Toothless is lettin' them mules drive theirselves!'

He was cursing the men as he sent his horse plunging on down into the gulch. Malone could almost feel relief at the comedy development. Still, he was worried about the tracks they had been following. Two riders hadn't made that wide circle of hard riding for nothing. Two drunken teamsters didn't change the basic danger.

He hadn't ridden twenty yards when he knew that his fears were well grounded. Two rifle shots banged almost in unison and he caught a glimpse through the brush of the toothless driver slumping in his seat, the reins falling to the heels of the nearest pair of mules. The other man toppled more slowly. Malone saw that he fell clear of the wagon and was scrambling to get clear of the wheels. Then brush cut off the view, and he drove hard in pursuit of Terpin, unable to hear the fat man's curses above the frantic braying of the frightened mules below them.

7

Malone dug in the spurs, catching a fleeting glimpse of the twin palls of gunsmoke that blossomed from the under-brush on the far side of the gulch trail. He was about to yell a warning to Terpin about the position of the ambushers when he saw that it wasn't necessary. Two men came running into view, one of them carrying what looked like a coil of rope at his shoulder. Even at the distance Malone recognized them. Tucker and Walt. So this was why the pair had been hanging around Muleskinner. Their job had been to stop this powder wagon.

He hit the last bit of slope. Terpin was already out in the open, but neither of the gunmen seemed to realize that they were about to be interrupted. Neither of them had thought to look up, and with the mules making so much noise, evidently they had not heard the hoofbeats on the mountain. At least they didn't hesitate. Tucker ran across to where the wounded guard was thrashing around. He pointed his six-gun calmly at the man's head and pulled the trigger. Then he hurried along to help Walt with the plunging mules.

The cold-blooded killing brought a fresh bellow of anger from Terpin, but neither of the killers seemed to hear him. They were fighting the mules to a halt, their backs to Terpin and Malone. It was evident that Terpin was going to hit the gulch floor a little in advance of the wagon, too quickly for the ambushers to reach their horses for a getaway. They would have to stand and fight — which they would do anyway. It wasn't likely that they would try to escape and leave witnesses to their crime.

Malone pulled the Sharps from its boot as he figured the timing. In seconds Terpin would be out in the open and the killers would see him. He was going to make a mighty big target for men who were evidently good hands with their guns. Malone knew that he had to make his own play so that he could give the furious Terpin a little help.

He picked his spot just as a yell of alarm from Tucker warned that the ambushers had finally seen the trouble that was coming on. Malone jumped from his horse without attempting to halt the animal, sliding into a position where he could steady the Sharps against a tree. Shots rang out in the gulch at the same instant, and he knew that Terpin was firing as he drove his horse straight at the gunmen. Walt promptly dropped to one knee, and Tucker ducked around to the rear of the wagon.

Malone was about to throw down on the kneeling Walt when he saw that Terpin was doing all right for himself. One of the fat man's slugs brought a yelp of pain, and Walt sagged to one side, his gun dropping from his hand.

Now Tucker was sighting from behind the wagon. Malone took quick aim and squeezed the trigger of the buffalo gun. One shot was enough.

When he reached the trail, not attempting to catch his winded horse, Terpin was shouting his anger. 'Ever see a dirtier bit o' killin'?' the fat man howled. 'Why'n hell did they have to kill them damned fools?'

Malone didn't bother to make a reply. It was pretty evident that the newest move on the part of the unknown enemy had been planned with a ruthlessness that was ample warning for the fnture. Scare talk was not going to be the weapon in the rest of this fight.

'Know 'em?' he asked Terpin.

'Nope.'

'It's the pair I told you about. They were with Hatfield at the Muleskinner Hotel. Been up here for a while, Guinn told me. Likely waiting for this powder to be moved.' He didn't add the obvious thought that they must have had advance knowledge of it.

He started past the dead Walt, curiously impressed that Terpin had scored a dead-center hit from the saddle. Either Matt had been mighty lucky or he was a hell of a man with a six-gun.

'Get the mules,' he called over his

shoulder. 'I want to see what that coil was that Tucker was carrying.'

That was when he made his almost-fatal mistake. Tucker hadn't moved since going down, and it seemed certain that the big Sharps slug had done its work. Malone had not reloaded the single-shot rifle, so when Tucker rolled fast, his gun coming up, Malone was caught with an empty weapon in his hand.

His moves were pure reflex. He went into a half crouch as he dropped the rifle, leaning a little to the right as his left hand swept down to the gun butt on his thigh. In the time it took Tucker to aim his gun, Malone drew and fired. The outlaw's gun blasted a split-second late, the slug going wild as it was triggered by the death convulsion. This time Tucker went down for keeps.

Behind him Malone heard the fat man's amazed howl. 'Godalmighty! That was the fastest goddam bit o' gunplay I ever seen!' Then he added, 'Make sure o' the bastard, Lefty. Like he done with that sonofabitch Beals.'

Malone didn't reply. He didn't want to encourage any talk about fast guns. He moved in grimly to stare down at the man he had killed. In a way it was pretty ridiculous. He didn't know this fellow but already he had had two brushes with him, the one at the corner of the hotel and now this. Maybe it was better that way. Tucker was nothing personal; he was just a hired gun who represented a force that had not yet been identified. There was no point in letting personal considerations enter in. It was enough to know that somebody had ordered a cold-blooded murder.

Malone took a good look at the coil that had fallen from Tucker's shoulder. It was a long length of the slow-burning type of fuse used in setting off blasting powder.

He ignored Terpin's excited questions and backtracked the ambushers to the timber from which they had cut down the two wagoners. As he had guessed, there were two horses picketed there, but a search of the saddlebags told him nothing. When he came back, Terpin was turning out the pockets of the dead men, his investigation no more enlightening than Malone's had been. The men had carried no evidence that would identify them or their employers. Not that it mattered. The whole deal was plain enough.

'One thing,' Terpin said, 'both o' the bastards had plenty money. Looka here.' He held up a sheaf of bank notes. 'Most likely they got their pay ahead o' time. Tens and twenties on the Mountain Bank of Denver. Somethin' fer Old Put to look into.'

'You got the main idea, I take it?' Malone asked, pointing to the coil of fuse. He wanted to keep the talk on the big problem and not let Terpin start any more talk about gun-play.

'Plain as the nose on yer face! They ambush our powder wagon here at the top o' the downgrade. Then they stick a fuse into a powder keg and light it. They wallop the mules a few licks and start 'em down the grade. Anywhere in the next quarter mile a blast knocks down half the cliff, and we've got to change the whole line. It's like I told you up there on the mountain.'

'You called it,' Malone agreed. 'But what's our next move? Do we try for a showdown now that we've nipped it?'

Terpin's round face took on a hint of mischief. 'Mebbe we oughta let 'em stew. Supposin' there ain't nothin' here but our dead men when the boys with the carts show up? We tell 'em we found the mules on the loose and our men murdered. No more. We could hide them dead sonsabitches under some rocks or somethin'.'

'Any reason for that?'

'Figger it out. What's important in this whole damned mess is time. Somebody's out to stop us from gittin' the line done this summer. We don't know who, but it don't figger no other way. So we git ourself some time.'

Malone nodded. 'We send the powder on with the tilt-up carts. All the men know is that somebody shot the powder-wagon men. And we don't go back to

Muleskinner for a day or so, and even then we don't talk about it. Hatfield has to make some guesses. He won't know what happened or anything about it. While he's figuring things out, we have a chance to make some progress — and to see if we can't come up with some facts.'

Terpin grinned. 'Yuh figger real good, Lefty. Almost as good as yuh handle a gun.'

'Let's get going.' It was no time to let Terpin start on that gun business. 'We've got an hour maybe to wipe out the sign and to get rid of a pair of dead skunks. Look around for a place to bury 'em; I'll blot the sign.'

Twenty minutes was enough for the job. The dead outlaws were dumped into a ravine where rocks could be rolled on top of them. The dead company men were loaded aboard the powder wagon for transportation to the upper camp and burial. Terpin wasted no sympathy on either of them. One had been in the employ of the enemy, and the other had been a troublemaker. Both had been drunk on the job. He would have dumped them into the hole with the two outlaws if he hadn't needed the bodies as part of the scene they were setting up.

The horses left in the brush by the ambushers posed another problem. Terpin wanted to dispose of them, but Malone advised against it. 'We've got new men coming along with the carts. They've been hearing a lot of talk about Indian threats. We can't let 'em think that the Utes are beginning to raid. The horses are evidence that this was done by white men.'

Terpin grunted. 'What difference does it make?'

'Plenty. Maybe we can get the men to think this was personal. One man was kinda unpopular, I take it. The other just came over to us from the enemy. Seems like you ought to be able to dream up something out of that. Just keep Indian talk out of it. We tell the men that we heard the shooting and scared the killers away before they could get to their horses. It's a better story to seep back to

Hatfield anyhow. He could imagine that his gunnies got lost in the mountains or that they're still trying for a crack at the blasting powder. Anything to make him hesitate is that much gain in time.'

'Yuh got it real good,' the fat man told him admiringly. 'Mebbe yuh're even better at makin' up lies than I am.'

They told the men Malone's story when the tilt-up carts came along. It was Terpin who supplied details that were not too different from the truth except for the story of the gun battle. Malone was glad that they had decided to lie. He didn't want any talk about his gun handling.

For the rest of the trip up the wagon trail, Malone and Terpin rode with the workmen. It seemed like a good idea to let the men get a feeling that they were being guarded, and Malone, at least, did a thorough scouting job along the way. He already knew that the dead ambushers had been alone when they made their circular approach to the gulch, but there was not yet any indication as to where

Hatfield and the black-bearded man might be. Possibly they were out ahead somewhere, waiting to check the results of the expected blast. Malone didn't propose to run across them without warning if he could avoid it.

The climb into the pass gave Malone a chance to study the terrain from a new angle. He could see how the rail line was going to avoid this grade by using the cliff top and winding around through the mountains. When they reached the pass itself, he could see how it would work out on the north side. Somewhere down below him was the valley where Old Put had made his big strike. Now the problem was to get the ore out of Silverdale and across the pass by a rail line. Without the railroad, it wouldn't pay to run the mine.

Suddenly he realized that this was the reason why the opposition could not be a freight-wagon outfit. Any experienced wagon man knew that wagons might make a profit out of the preliminary stages of a mine development. Mine owners would work without profit in order to get things going. But they wouldn't continue operating that way for long. Wagons simply didn't permit a profit. A rail line had to reach the mine or the mine wasn't worth working. Guinn knew it. So would any legitimate buyer. This opposition to the railroad — now showing murderous inclinations — had to be something more than wagon competition. He wondered what other explanation could be found.

On the far side of the pass, the wagon trail ran practically parallel to the line that had been surveyed for the railroad. Terpin pointed out the one stretch where the rails would make a long loop to avoid a steep grade, indicating what the upper camp gang was expected to do in the way of saving time on the total job.

Malone already knew that it had been Terpin's idea to work from both ends at the same time. The second camp had been set up late in the previous summer so the grading had come out only some three miles from the mines. Now the hope was that this crew could reach the pass summit in time to meet Flannery's gang at that point. A rail-laying gang would follow close on the heels of Flannery's graders, and they could push forward in a hurry when they found the extra miles of graded roadbed ahead of them.

They were discussing the prospects and the time budget when Terpin suddenly said, 'I been thinkin' about that gun play o' yourn. Somehow it seemed like somethin' I heard about.'

'Forget it. I'd say that your shooting from the saddle was a better bit of gun handling than mine.'

Terpin was not to be sidetracked. 'It ain't the shootin' I'm talkin' about. It's the way yuh got that gun out so goddam fast. I never heard of but one man could do it like that. Feller name of Jack Kyle.'

Malone braced himself even though he didn't look around. He could sense from the fat man's tone that there was a lot behind the words. 'This Kyle a friend of yours?' he inquired casually.

'Nope. Never seen him but once, kind of in a crowd. But that was enough. There was a hard case busted into this rail camp where Kyle was actin' as a kind of marshal fer the railroad people. He'd been braggin' around that he aimed to git Kyle — jest to let the world know that there was somebody faster'n Kyle was supposed to be. Kyle let the bastard make the first move and then plugged him plumb center before the gunnie ever got his hammer back. Fastest thing I ever seen — 'til today.'

'Lots of fast guns around,' Malone said. 'Have to be. They get killed off in a hurry because they're everybody's target. Seems like the more of 'em get killed, the more keep comin' along.'

'That's how it was with Kyle, I reckon. Plenty gun hawks tried to take him in a stand-up fight, but it was finally bush-whackers what got him. Up in Wyomin' somewhere, I heard.' Again the odd tone was in the fat man's voice He was definitely prodding, looking for a reaction.

Malone became deliberately casual. 'It

happens often. I guess this Pyle wasn't the only one it happened to.'

'The name was Kyle. Where'n hell have yuh been all yer life that yuh never heard of him! He ramrodded a couple o' the toughest railhead towns in Kansas.'

Malone shrugged. 'Like I said, plenty of gunmen in the world. Maybe too damned many.'

'Not like Jack Kyle. There's a hell of a lot o' loose talk about two gun men out here in the West, and mostly it's jest a lot of gab fer the dudes to write home about. Ain't one man in a hunnert kin handle one gun and make a halfway decent job of it, so most of 'em don't try to git gay with a pair o' hawglegs. Likely they'd git all tangled up and shoot theirselves in the leg if'n they tried. But this here Jack Kyle was a real two-hander. They got a word fer it. Amphibious, or somethin' like that. Didn't make no difference which hand he used — or he could use 'em both at once. And good.'

'Sounds interesting,' Malone said, his voice hinting that it really wasn't.

'Yuh're damned right. Ain't no end to the yarns they tell about him. One feller I knowed claimed that he seen Kyle git trapped by four gunnies that had swore to kill him. He gunned all four of 'em and didn't git a scratch out of it. Two bullets outa each of his guns and there was four dead sidewinders. He was hell on wheels, all right!'

'I must have missed something — but somehow I never knew anybody named Kyle.' In a way that was strictly the truth.

'He was a real dude, too,' Terpin went on. 'Young feller — about the same size and build as yerself. Always sported a long black mustache and a goatee. Big ivory gun butt on each hip, a pair of shiny Texas boots and a hat that musta cost forty dollars. Even in a cowtown where a clean face made a man look like a sissy, this here Kyle stood around lookin' like somethin' out of a pitcher book. And nobody dared say boo about it. He was a heller!'

'And he got himself killed.'

'That's the way I heard it. I was

gradin' fer the Santa Fe by that time, so I didn't git none o' the details. Some time after that I heard that a feller they was hangin' fer another job admitted that him and his partner dry-gulched Kyle and murdered him.'

'That's the way of it,' Malone said. 'Sooner or later they get it. Right now I'm wondering how that polecat Hatfield has lived so long. Sure as hell he don't deserve to.'

'Mebbe his luck's about to run out. If'n we find out fer sure that he was back o' that bushwhackin' this mornin', I'll sure as hell try to make sure that he don't do many more jobs!'

The upper camp came into view, and Terpin dropped back to bawl orders at the men handling the tilt-up carts. They had to leave the wagon road and climb a short but steep grade to the proposed rail line. Matt was busy for the next few minutes, making sure that weary animals made the grade, and it gave Malone time to think. Terpin had hammered the Jack Kyle subject a little too much for comfort. When a sharp fellow like Terpin got an idea into his head, it might be difficult to keep him from following it up.

Malone had a strong urge to get out of the whole business before any such trouble could develop. Jack Kyle had to stay dead. It was hardly worth getting a railroad built if the price was the revival of Kyle.

Even with the thought, he knew that he didn't really mean it. This rail line was his own big play for a new life, but the line would mean more to Old Put than to anyone else. And he owed Putnam plenty. The risk was going to be unpleasant, but at least it was Terpin who was now the cause of concern, not Hatfield or Tillie Atherton. Somehow Malone was beginning to feel pretty good about Matt Terpin. The fat man was all right.

8

They found the upper camp in somewhat the same state of readiness that had been the case at the lower end of Muleskinner Gulch. The skeleton crew that had come in as soon as winter broke had been getting a lot done, repairing frost damage and relocating a couple of drains that had not proved equal to the strain of carrying off the spring freshets. Shawn O'Boyle, a brawny, redfaced man of about fifty, evidently knew his business and was wasting no time. He didn't handle his men with the easy good humor that was Flannery's method, but morale seemed to be good. Most of his gang came out to look at the new carts, and Malone had a feeling that with just a little encouragement they would use the scant hour before nightfall in trying them out, the way a child would try out a new toy.

Malone and Terpin took O'Boyle into

their confidence in the matter of the ambushing. It was agreed that the story given to the new men would be told to anyone else — except Hannibal Putnam and possibly his daughter. It would be interesting to see whether Jim Hatfield would take any steps to locate his missing gunmen. Terpin hoped that he would; he wanted very much to connect Hatfield with the killings.

Malone felt relieved when the session with O'Boyle was over. They had told the big Irishman about the fight, but Terpin had not dwelled on Malone's fast draw. Terpin had been content to report it simply as a quick duel between Malone and the wounded gunman, not even mentioning that Tucker had been ready to fire before Malone even went for his gun. And he seemed happy to brag about his own prowess in knocking over the other outlaw in the opening attack. Malone even helped him with his boasting. Better that than more talk about Jack Kyle.

For the first time in months, Malone's

mind kept coming back to the subject. It wasn't something that a man could forget entirely, but lately he had been remembering only in a stolid sort of way, thinking about it as something that was all over. Now he knew some of the old misgivings.

It annoyed him a little to recall Terpin's description of the swaggering young idiot who had called himself Jack Kyle. He had picked the name because he thought it sounded like the proper name for a fast gun — and because he didn't think 'Arthur Malone' carried the proper ring of deadliness. For much the same kind of immature reason, he had cultivated that elaborate mustache and goatee, keeping them carefully dyed black because sandy whiskers weren't dramatic enough. There was no doubt about it; he had been a pretty asinine young man, intensely proud of his skill with a gun and determined to become a legend.

It helped a little to remember that he had never used his skill on the wrong side of the law — and he had never gone out of his way to invite trouble. After his first few fights, that had not been necessary. There were always challengers who wanted to pick up a quick reputation by killing a man like Jack Kyle. He had been firmly trapped in a situation that he had deliberately contrived before he grew up enough to realize what his life had become. By that time there was no way out. He had to keep meeting those ambitious young fools, the fools who wanted to be the same kind of idiot he had made of himself. Running away would not be any answer. Somebody would hunt him down. There was no such thing as a retired gun hawk.

His thoughts went back to that sweltering July afternoon in the Wyoming alkali country. The trail of the stagecoach bandits had led into badlands where even the Sioux didn't venture. Malone — Kyle — had followed at a fast pace, assuming that the outlaws would try to get through the bad stretch as rapidly as possible. It was an assumption that almost cost him his life. The bandits turned smart, dry-gulching him where their trail led between two of the chalky buttes that dotted the country. The first bushwhack shot broke his right arm and spooked his bronc. Maybe that was why he was still alive; the gunmen had not been able to sight on a good target after the horse began his bucking run.

Malone didn't know how long he had managed to stay in the saddle, but it was long enough so that the horse was plenty bloody when it was found a few days later. The bandits made one attempt to finish him off as he lay on the sunbaked ground, but he roused to semi-consciousness long enough to drive them off with his left-hand gun. He had only a dim memory of the things he did in a painful daze after that. He knew that somehow he had stopped the bleeding and had bound the broken arm to his side. The rest of it had never become clear. All he knew for sure was that a prospector named Hannibal Putnam had found him and had taken care of him. Putnam had been taking a short cut through the badlands on his way to the Bighorn foothills.

The next few weeks Malone remembered clearly enough. There had been no regular doctor within miles, but Putnam had done a remarkably good job on the arm. Malone was a semi-crippled partner by the time the pair of them began to search the Bighorns for gold. The arm was healing well, but Malone didn't try very hard to restore it to normal use. He could do just as well with his left hand, and it pleased him to think that this was his chance to see the end of Jack Kyle, the two-gun man. Lefty Art Malone would certainly be an improvement on Kyle.

Finally he told the entire story to Putnam, explaining why he wanted to lose his old identity. Hannibal Putnam sympathized and the pair began to think of themselves as partners. Malone had been carrying a fair sum of money on him at the time of the injury, and Putnam needed a grub-stake. With Malone supplying the funds and Old Put visiting the towns to make the necessary purchases, they managed to work their way into Montana, where they finally made a strike that was worth something.

By that time they knew that Kyle's blood-stained horse had been found running loose. Several months later they heard that a convicted outlaw had confessed to the killing of Jack Kyle. It seemed to set things up. Malone's right hand was now as good as new, but in the interval he had formed the habit of using the left most of the time, so it was a simple matter for him to become Lefty Malone. As an added precaution he remained at the Montana diggings until Hannibal Putnam's sudden prosperity and ambition ran into trouble.

Malone was reluctant to come back to a railroad construction job. There was too much risk of meeting men he had known in his earlier days. And he particularly did not like the idea of coming along as a trouble hunter for a railroad project. That was exactly what he had been in the days when he was a kid gone wild for gun-glory. Only for Hannibal Putnam would he take the risk. If anyone discovered that Lefty Malone was really Jack Kyle — or the other way around — there would be the same old problem. Some fool would insist on trying his skill against the known speed of Kyle. Malone knew that he had to find some way of throwing Terpin off the scent. The man was too much of a loudmouth to trust with that kind of secret.

He did not sleep too well that night, but he was up early enough to go out with Terpin and O'Boyle for a look at the blasting project. The snow was almost gone even here on the mountain, and O'Boyle's men were to begin the same kind of preliminary work that Flannery had been doing for nearly a week. While they waited for the thaw that would permit real digging, they would move ahead with the blasting job. The thing had been well planned to save as much time as possible against the day when a delay might prove ruinous, and Malone found himself admiring the way it had been worked out.

They were well up along the face of the slope beyond the graded strip before he remembered the two horses they had brought in to camp. It also occurred to him that there had been no further mention of the money that Terpin had taken from the bodies of the dead ambushers. At the time Malone had not been much interested. He hadn't been concerned over either money or horses. He didn't want either. Even in his deadlier days Kyle had never taken a profit out of killing. Malone didn't propose to start it now.

He asked Terpin about the horses and got a broad grin in reply. 'No worries there,' the fat man assured him 'Shawn's got a feller who's a real smart hombre with a runnin' iron. We ain't goin' to git picked up fer hoss stealin'.'

'What happens to the horses after the brands are changed?'

'That part yuh'll like. Our hunters kin use 'em. I told yuh that we been workin' a meat-huntin' game all along — not that yer little stunt wasn't smart enough. Anyhow, Shawn gives the huntin' jobs to the men what work best ever week. They git to be hunters fer the next week. It keeps 'em keen, and they bring in a hell of a lot o' meat.'

Malone laughed. 'You've got it worked out better than the way Hannibal and I dreamed it up.' He decided not to ask about the money. Either Terpin would come up with another good explanation or . . . Maybe it was just as well not to press the point. Terpin was a good man in his own peculiar way, and Malone was ready to concede a bit of minor thievery to keep the man going in the right direction. In a game like this one, there was no point in getting too careful about a man's honesty.

For the balance of the trip Malone left most of the talking to Terpin and O'Boyle. The big Irishman was serious now, discussing the exact details of how the blasting could be done so as to leave a minimum of grading to be done when the blast was finished. He had brought drillers along with him on the trip up the mountain, and the men went to work without delay. Malone noted that for the most part the fat man stayed out of the way, leaving O'Boyle to run the job. Twice O'Boyle came over to ask for advice, but Terpin offered none unless he was asked for it. The two men seemed to understand each other pretty well.

Malone watched with satisfaction as the drilling began, then rode away while Terpin and O'Boyle were planning their attack on the second of the two rock spurs. It was their job. They knew what to do about it, and Malone wanted them to feel that he was not sticking around to be critical. There was also the matter of his own responsibility. He had to make sure that the construction men would not be subject to any sort of attack. Since he did not know what Hatfield had done after sending the ambushers out, he had to take a few precautions.

He added a third reason as he left the drill gang. By keeping some distance between himself and Terpin, he left no chance for any more talk about Jack Kyle.

He spent half of the day in a sweep of the mountain slopes north of the pass, convincing himself that there was as yet nothing in the area to warrant any concern. He could find no sign, Indian or otherwise, even though there was still enough snow so that tracks would be easy to spot.

That night the talk around camp was strictly business. O'Boyle spent some time with his gang bosses, trying to figure out the most efficient ways of using the new grading carts. The men had tried them out in the small sections where the ground had thawed sufficiently, but there had been no chance to give them a real test. They looked good, and the general opinion was that they would save a lot of time.

Terpin went over the blasting plans with O'Boyle, issuing careful orders about both the drilling and the placing of the powder charges. 'It's got to be a good clean job, Shawn,' he said soberly.

'Blow the rock right, and there won't be much gradin' to do. Make a mess of it, and we'll lose a week. Keep it in mind; we got to make every minute count.'

It was agreed that Terpin would leave on the following morning, depending on O'Boyle to get the blasting job done. The fat man proposed to ride back to Muleskinner along the wagon trail, hoping that he could pick up some information along the line. A couple of Guinn's wagons had come up the trail past the camp during the day, so it seemed likely that the regular wagon traffic would be moving. There should be some word of how Hatfield was reacting. He ought to be getting worried at not hearing from his hired thugs. Maybe he would make a wrong move or two. Terpin hoped loudly that he would.

Meanwhile, Malone was to start doing what had first appeared to be his principal duty, looking for the signs of trouble that those early rumors had suggested. He would scout the country south and east of the pass with considerable thoroughness, trying to determine whether there was actually any chance of conflict with the Indians. If the rail really encroached on territory sacred to the Utes, there would be trouble, but if the whole thing had been a wild tale aimed simply at scaring workmen, he wanted to know it.

There would be another object in view, he realized. Somebody had done a piece of scouting before Tucker and Walt set out to lay their ambush. The pair had used a round about route to the ambush scene, covering most of it in darkness. Malone wanted to backtrack them, if the trail could still be found, hoping to get some hint as to where they had traveled. Perhaps other attempts at stopping construction might use such a route. A man never went wrong in knowing everything possible about the enemy.

He spent two full days at the job, camping in the mountains at night. There was no great difficulty in locating the trail Tucker and Walt had left behind them, but that was all he could learn from his hours of search. He had range in both directions from the line of survey, using particular care when the line swung east in its long climbing loop to the pass. There was nothing to indicate that Indians used this country for anything, ceremonial or otherwise. He didn't even find any hint that the Utes did much hunting in this part of the mountains.

The trail of the bushwackers was almost as barren of result. The pair had known the country well enough to make a circuit that let them reach their ambush without leaving tracks in the gulch mud. Malone couldn't see that there was any more to it than that. There was no well-beaten track, no suggestion that anyone was using the hills for any other purpose.

He was a little discouraged when he rode down toward the railhead camp in late afternoon. Then he saw how much progress Flannery had made in three days, and he felt better. This was what counted. His own part in the operation was pretty much a negative kind of thing. He couldn't do much to push the line into the mountains; all he could hope for was that he could let Flannery and his gang do it.

And they were doing it. With the enemy temporarily off balance from the failure of their big attempt at real dirt work, Flannery had made good use of the time. Both grade and track were well into Muleskinner Gulch, gaining altitude for the real climb. At the rate they were going — weather and an unknown enemy permitting — they'd have track in the mountains within a week.

Terpin was openly triumphant when Malone found him at the warehouse. 'Yer friend Hatfield has been runnin' around like a hen with its head cut off,' he greeted. 'Made two trips up the gulch with Guinn's wagons, claimin' he's jest out to git some exercise. Both times he went as far as the cliff and then he pottered around and rode back. Ain't much doubt but what he knowed what them bastards was tryin' to do. Mebbe I'd oughta shoot him now and have it over. Ain't no doubt but what he was the sonofabitch what give the orders fer them killin's.'

'Better take it easy,' Malone advised. 'No point in getting all mixed up with the law. Anyway, it's time we're after. While he's wasting time being confused, we're working. Right?'

'I reckon so. But I'd sure as hell like to bust him good.'

'Don't get careless. This Hatfield is a fast man with a gun.'

'Fast as Jack Kyle?' Terpin asked, his smile a little awry.

'I wouldn't know. But Hatfield has quite a reputation.'

The fat man let it go. 'Changed orders fer the train crew,' he said. 'They'll lay over here instead of at the Junction now. With Flannery pushin' up the gulch so damned fast, we need the engine to shove supplies up behind him.'

Malone nodded. 'I saw that there were a couple of carloads of rail up at the end of the track.'

'Got a system,' Terpin bragged. 'In the mornin's the train keeps shovin' stuff

9

Malone had a good hour to relax and to enjoy the feeling that everything was going well. He ate supper in the mess shack, joining Terpin and Flannery. They talked about the progress that had been made, about the way Jim Hatfield was showing his frustration, about the chances that the line could be completed on schedule. It had to be careful talk, particularly because of the way Terpin had to be hushed every so often. Not that it made much difference; Flannery's crew made so much noise that no one could have overheard anything like ordinary sounds.

They had come up with a new verse to *Flannery's Wake* and were teaching it to the new hands. Again it appeared to be partly one of the original bits of the song, with alterations adapting it to the gang's determination to make tee-totaler Flannery sound like a drunkard.

Now Flannery worked on a railroad
    line.
At swingin' a hammer there's no
    one like.
But gut full o' whisky and feelin' fine
He walloped hisself instead of a
    spike.
We wrapped him up in a nice clean
    sheet,
And laid him out upon his bed,
Wid a gallon o' pop-skull at his feet,
And a barrel o' praties at his head.

Wid me philalloo, hubbaboo, whack
    hurroo, boys,
Didn't we sing 'til our jaws did ache,
And shout and laugh and drink and
    sing,
Oh, it's lots of fun at Flannery's
    wake.

Terpin grimaced at the stoop-shouldered grade boss. 'I'd like to see them
monkeys git gay like that with Shawn
O'Boyle. He'd bust some heads.'
    Flannery laughed. 'And lose men

from the job. I ain't a-mindin', long as they work.'

The squeal of the locomotive whistle brought a quick end to the supper hilarity. Everybody went out to watch the train come up from Fremont Junction, and the sight added to Malone's feeling that this was the real thing. What had happened out there in the gulch was just something that was not actually a part of the picture. A train coming up the grade. Men going out to satisfy their curiosity by watching it arrive. This was normal. He hoped it would stay that way.

He saw that Isabel Putnam had come out to stand some distance away from the track. She was alone, and he left it that way. He was not sure just how much she knew or what she ought to be told. Then he saw Mark Wheeler watching from in front of the office. Wheeler also was alone, his expression hard to interpret.

Flannery commented, 'Looks like Wheeler's got a burr up his tail. He don't know what in hell he's supposed to do next.'

'Mebbe we kin keep it that way,' Terpin growled, 'No body to give him orders since Hatfield ain't sure o' nothin' Yuh got yer man keepin' an eye on him, Denny?'

'Yep. And on that hostler. We got 'em dead to right. Name the day and we'll turn 'em inside out.'

Terpin jerked a blunt thumb at Malone. 'Boss man holdin' back. Mebbe he's right.'

Malone did not comment.

The passengers who came down from the rickety old coach were a mixed lot, much as had been the case when Malone himself had made the trip. As yet there had been no attempt to organize passenger service. The work train was used to bring in workmen, and others could ride simply by paying a small fee to the company agent at the junction. To Malone it had seemed a bit ironic that some of the passengers being carried at the low fare were coming in to stop further development of the line.

He saw perhaps two dozen workmen coming out of the front end of the car, and Flannery went to meet them and direct them to the company office, where Wheeler and the clerks waited. Then he saw the little man who was following them. Hannibal Putnam was playing it big, waving his new men out ahead of him. Malone wasn't quite sure what the act meant, but one look at Putnam's outfit and he knew that the wizened little fellow was up to something. After months of working with Old Put and seeing him in faded Levis and a ragged shirt, it was quite a jolt to encounter the enormous Texas hat, the well-tailored frock coat, the white linen, and the shiny boots. It seemed likely that the old man might adopt such a rig to impress the Denver bankers, but the outfit looked a bit ridiculous at Muleskinner. Possibly Putnam was counting on that fact. Maybe he wanted somebody to think of him as a pompous little man who might be taken rather lightly.

The thought made Malone turn his

attention to the other end of the car, where another lot of passengers had appeared. A few roughly clad men swung over to follow the workmen toward the S. & F. office, but two others headed straight across the valley toward the wagon camp. Malone studied them as closely as possible from his angle. One seemed oddly familiar as they picked their way across the dried ruts.

Then Malone caught a gesture from Putnam. The little man was calling his attention to the newcomers. Malone turned to look again, studying the garb as well as the outlines from the rear. It struck him that they were dressed much as Tucker and Fredericks had been, but for a moment it escaped him that the boots and jackets hinted at surveyors of some sort. Then he knew that he had seen the bandy legs of the shorter man before. The fellow had run a transit for the Kansas Pacific until being fired for getting into a drunken brawl, a brawl that Jack Kyle had ended simply by appearing on the scene and looking deadly.

Putnam reached him, extending a thin, wiry hand and offering a wry grin that showed missing molars. 'Keep an eye on that pair, Lefty. I got reason to think they're up here to make trouble.'

'I hope you know who sent them. That's the big difficulty right now. We don't know who we're fightin'.'

Putnam let one wrinkled eyelid droop. 'I'm gittin' some ideas, Lefty. Tonight we'll talk it out.'

'Make it tonight. Don't say anything around the office.'

The little man's wryly humorous expression changed abruptly. 'Ain't havin' no trouble with Isabel, are you?'

'No. But I'll give you odds that your bright boy Wheeler is taking pay from the opposition. Anything he hears goes right over to Jim Hatfield. You know about him, I guess.'

'I been hearin'. Let me get some grub under my belt, and then come over to what passes fer home.' He turned to Terpin. 'I want you in on this, Matt.'

'And Flannery,' Malone added.

'Who's runnin' this?' Putnam demanded. 'Oh, all right. Have it your way. You will, anyhow.' He didn't sound half as gruff as he was trying to.

It was something over an hour later that the meeting began in the rough little room that passed as a sitting room for Isabel and her aunt. Hannibal Putnam took a chair behind the plank table, whose bareness was hidden by a blanket. He was still wearing the big hat, but the tight expression around his eyes hinted that he was no longer trying for any theatrical effect. Old Put had trouble an' he knew it.

Isabel and her aunt occupied the only other chairs in the room, having pulled them up to the table on Putnam's right. Terpin was spread out — as only Terpin could spread — on a settee that creaked warningly under his bulk. Malone and Flannery occupied camp chairs against the wall.

It occurred to Malone that this was an odd collection of people to be working together on any project, particularly the building of a railroad into the mountains.

An old prospector who had struck it rich and was getting carried away by the idea of being a promoter and financier. His daughter whose Eastern education had been good but not for the kind of job she was now trying to handle. An old maid who had never quite reconciled herself to leaving New England. Two roustabout construction men, one of them with all the gentle instincts of a Sicilian bandit. And a reformed gun-slinger who was trying to keep his violent past under cover. It was scarcely the kind of group that would be picked for the job they were trying to do.

Almost with the thought he realized that they had something in common — determination. Putnam wanted to prove that he could develop the Silverdale mines without having to turn to outside interests to expand the workings and build the railroad. Isabel wanted to see her father succeed. Terpin and Flannery had a financial interest in getting the job done, probably the first financial interest either had ever had in a construction project. For himself, Malone knew that his interest was something more than monetary. Somehow he couldn't work up much interest in making profits — although he didn't try to tell himself that this wasn't a point to be considered. He kept thinking in terms Old Put's ambitions. It was Putnam who had doctored his arm and taken him along on the prospect trail. It was Putnam who knew the truth about him and who kept quiet, evidently understanding the younger man's desire to break clean with the old identity. One way or another — maybe in more than one way — Putnam had saved his life. It was reason enough for Malone to be concerned with building Putnam's railroad.

The little man opened the meeting almost grimly. 'I know we got a lot o' facts to swap back and forth — and we'll get to that — but first I want to make sure that all of you know a few things that maybe I shoulda told you when we first got together on this deal. The most important one is that we're tryin' to operate on a shoestring. I ain't the smart financial wizard I kinda figured myself to be, so we're out on a limb. And that explains a lot of the mess you folks are tryin' to handle. There's people what would like to saw off that limb we're on.'

'The same ones who cooked up the Ute talk?' Malone asked.

'Right. Injun talk didn't make sense. Neither did the hint that our big enemy was Brian Guinn. It had to be somebody hidin' behind them two ideas. But let me tell it my way.

'I was kinda short o' cash after I opened up that new shaft at Silverdale. The new strike made a rail line a smart investment, but I didn't have nothin' to invest. First I set up a corporation, as you know. Right now there's about forty stockholders, most of 'em our own workmen. I own a bit over forty per cent. Isabel owns another five. The other fifty-five was taken up by the men who're doin' the actual work. You all know about that.' He grinned as he caught Malone's questioning glance. 'I didn't put it right,

I reckon. My forty per cent is a partnership deal, like the Montana property and the Silverdale diggings. What I hold is half Malone's. But that's neither here nor there. This corporation money didn't much more than buy us some materials and the second-hand rollin' stock we're usin'. I had to float bonds to get the job movin'. It takes a hell of a lot o' money to build a railroad.'

'What kind of bonds?' Isabel asked, speaking for the first time since entering the room. It had seemed to Malone that she resented meeting with himself and the construction bosses, but now he decided that she was simply being reserved because she realized that this was a serious matter.

'Short-termers,' her father said grimly. 'That's where I let the world know that I ain't nothin' more than a prospector down underneath. I had it all planned out that we'd be makin' money outa the mines and the railroad by mid-summer. That was the way the surveyors talked. So I tried to save a few dollars with bonds that come due in late September and early October of this year.'

'Who bought the bonds?' Malone asked.

'A variety of folks. But it seems like most o' the buyers have sold out — for one reason or another. Right now it looks like most o' the bonds are held by the Mountain Bank in Denver.'

He grinned crookedly as he added, 'Seems like the name means somethin' to you. Any of you happen to know who runs the Mountain Bank?'

'Polecats,' Terpin growled. Then he added, 'Only dunno what names they use.'

Putnam grimaced. 'No argument on that. It seems the the Mountain Bank was organized by a couple o' gents with plenty of money. Names are Burchell and Hatfield.'

'Hatfield!' Malone exclaimed. 'How'd he get hold enough money to run a bank? He was never anything but a hired gun!'

'Seems like he hired out to the right man,' Putnam told him dryly. 'Nobody ever proved anything on 'em, but there's talk. The general idea is that this here Burchell was fixin' to swindle a miner — stupid feller like me, I reckon — outa his property. The sucker got smart, and Hatfield picked a fight with him and killed him. That left Burchell with a stranglehold on the mine. Nobody can prove that was all planned that way, but anyhow Burchell and Hatfield went into partnership and started the Mountain Bank.

'Now it makes sense,' Malone growled. 'Stolen money based on swindle and murder. Now Hatfield fits.'

'Yuh know him?' Putnam asked.

'Sure. That's part of what we need to tell you — after you get your part of the yarn finished.'

'Ain't much more to mine. This here Mountain Bank outfit is sure as hell fixin' to take over the railroad line. Come October they can do it — if we can't find a way to make the bond payments.'

'But if the line's operating by that time?'

'That's the whole point. I figure we'll be able to pay off or get new backing if we can show operating profit by the end of August. Which is what this is all about. Burchell and Hatfield plan to keep us tied up. Then we don't get the line done — because men are afraid of Injuns or because they block supplies.'

'Or because they blast our line right out from under us,' Terpin added.

That needed explanation, so the story of the ambush was told, only the details of the gun battle being passed over. Malone could see the horror on Isabel Putnam's face as she learned about the affair. It seemed to him that she was shocked more by the callous way the dead outlaws had been buried than by the cold-blooded murder of the wagoners.

'So we got that little bit o' monkey business stopped cold,' Terpin concluded. 'We're movin' fast from both ends. Plenty supplies on hand. Mebbe we ain't got so much to worry about.'

'Let's figure a mite,' Putnam nodded.

'How long do you boys calculate it'll take to get the line through — providin' we don't get hit by no Ute raids, outlaw blastin' jobs, or late-season blizzards?'

'Three weeks to the pass,' Flannery put in. 'Another week across the hump. Two more down the grade with rails into Silverdale. This is the second day of May. About the third week of June we oughta be able to run a train from one end o' the line to the other.'

'Add a week,' Terpin said shortly. 'Denny's a damned optimist.' He bobbed his heavy head in apology toward Isabel. 'And don't forget chances of some washouts with storms. We lost some roadbed durin' the winter when we didn't figure our drainage right. Can't tell how these here mountain streams is gonna run when we git a real hard rain.'

'You still figure for a finish some time about the first of July?' Putnam inquired.

'That's about it.'

'If we can do it, we're in good shape. And Burchell will be licked. I reckon you know what that means?'

'Sure,' Malone growled. 'It means that they've got at least one dirty trick still in the works. We can figure that they'll work out two or three extra.'

'What makes you so sure?' Isabel demanded. 'You speak as though you had knowledge of their plans.'

Malone didn't let her tone bother him. 'Sometimes I'm practically brilliant,' he told her solemnly. 'This time it didn't take too much horse sense. Matt says that if everything thing goes at top speed and we don't have any bad weather, accidents, or interference, we'll have a train running by the first of July. At the other end of the picture there's the deadline that we just heard about. To show a profit that would encourage refinancing by the end of August, we have to have trains running on schedule not later than the middle of the month — and that's cutting it pretty fine. Anyway, let's figure that we've got six weeks margin.'

'Sounds right,' Putnam cut in. 'I like to hear it that way.'

'Don't get too enthusiastic. That's

the maximum. Every little bit of trouble cuts it down. The point is that Burchell's crowd will make guesses just about like ours. They know as much about it as we do. Maybe more. Anyway, they've planned to get rid of those six weeks. Maybe they didn't expect our construction gangs to get on the job so promptly, so they might have planned to kill only five weeks.'

'Now you're becoming rather technical,' Isabel scoffed.

Malone grinned. 'Brilliant again. I figure that the Ute talk was stirred up to make a bit of delay at the start. If we didn't get men in here, we couldn't get a jump on the season. All right, so we've beat that game. We don't have full crews yet, but the men already on the job have made a better start than we could have hoped for. That's what gives us the six weeks. I think the opposition might have figured five weeks and maybe the Ute talk trimming it to four. So we're two weeks to the good on them.'

'You should have been a lawyer.'

Again he ignored the tone. 'Now go ahead with that kind of guessing. They likely figured that busting the cliff down would account for another two weeks. Matt said it would have meant two or three. That still leaves a bit of time not yet accounted for. That's why I said we'd have to expect more trouble. They wouldn't leave the job half undone.'

Immediately, they were all in the discussion, finally agreeing that Malone had figured it out pretty accurately. It was Malone who broke it up, firing a question at Putnam.

'How did you get on to Burchell? The last I heard, you still hadn't picked up any hint as to who was out to break us.'

'Things kept addin' up,' the little man said with a wry grin. 'I found out that the Mountain Bank was buyin' up our bonds whenever they could lay their hands on 'em. So I started checkin' into the outfit. I already told you what I found out. I had a man watchin' the bank, tryin' to find out who might be gettin' cozy with Burchell. Before long this Grimes showed up — about the time I got your letter tellin' me who he was and what he was doin' up here at Muleskinner. Things got real clear after that.'

'And you know something about the pair who came up on the train with you tonight? I thought you gave me the signal to look 'em over.'

'All I know is that they went to see Burchell twice this week. Seemed like a fair hint that they might be the next move in the game.'

'I think you're imagining too much,' Isabel said with a fresh show of annoyance. 'You make a lot of guesses, but none of them even begin to explain how these supposed enemies hope to profit by ruining our railroad. What would they want with a ruined railroad?'

Hannibal Putnam looked helplessly at the men. 'See what comes of givin' a female a education?' he asked. 'Head full o' stuff and none of it makin' sense! Iz, they ain't figurin' to ruin this railroad. Even blastin' the cliff wouldn't ruin the line. Property's still here. Chance of profits still here. All that gets ruined is *us*. If we can't pay off our bonds, they step in and grab everything as creditors. It would sure as hell work out that they'd get almost a ready-made railroad for what it's costin' 'em to ruin us. That's real cheap.'

'Then they would run it?'

'Mebbe. I also got some hints that they've got a silent partner in on the deal. Feller's some kind of director or somethin' of the Denver and Rio Grande. With our line sort of a spur of the D.R.G., it wouldn't take much politickin' to have the D.R.G. buy up the S. & F. With one o' their directors pushin' the thing along, they'd likely pay plenty for it. That's the big chance of profit for Burchell and Hatfield. Or maybe they plan to run it theirselves. It'd pay. The mines are goin' good.' He shook his head as he added, 'Hell of it is that we likely lose the mines if we lose the railroad. I got things into a hell of a mess tryin' to find enough dollars.'

'No two ways about it,' Terpin grumbled. 'They got to stop us or lose their ante. We got to stop 'em from stoppin' us or we lose ours. They ain't stopped at murder, so we kin look fer more o' the same.'

'But can't the law do something about such tactics?' she insisted. 'You say that the Mountain Bank was organized with funds that were the products of fraud and murder. Now that bank is paying for more murder. I should think that we could . . .'

'You ain't back in Massachusetts now,' the little man told her. 'We can't prove a thing. And we don't have any time to play around with lawsuits that wouldn't help. It's just a simple case of keeping them off our necks while we get the job done. If we push the line through, they take a licking. They know it. They've already spent a lot of money on stopping us, and they won't want to lose either that investment or the chance of making a profit by taking over the line.'

That was where the session might just as well have ended. They thrashed things out for another hour, but the situation remained just as it had been. Terpin and his men were to keep right on driving, trying for a rate of progress that would give them a little leeway in case of bad weather or accident. Malone was to spend his time keeping them clear of dirty work. There was only one decision reached. Mark Wheeler was to get the sack. They decided not to charge him with the betrayal that they could not prove. It would be simply a case of telling him that they didn't need him any longer. Putnam was going to stay at the Muleskinner base, no longer having any reason for working out of Denver. He would take charge of the office. That part Isabel didn't seem to like, but her father didn't pay any attention to her protest. He was obviously taking Malone and Terpin as his authorities. If they said Wheeler was a spy, that was enough for him.

'So let's get at it,' the little man concluded. 'Either we make a pot o' money together or we all go busted together. Keep it in mind.'

Malone wasn't so sure that it was as simple as that for him. He was silent as he walked beside Terpin to their sleeping quarters in the warehouse. Somehow he wasn't at all sure that money was what had brought him into this deal. Building a railroad was a big thing. He had been part of railroad building in the earlier years, but always he had been a curiously detached part of it, simply a law officer who tried to keep the riotous elements under control at railhead camps. Now he hoped to do a little more than that. It was hard to see how his job was much different from the one Jack Kyle had worked — but he liked to think that this time he was doing something a little more significant.

10

Next day it was easy to imagine that the only problems were the routine ones connected with mountain terrain. Flannery's men went out singing. Now they rode flatcars, as the distance between living quarters and work site increased. The little engine puffed its way up the grade with materials and men. The snow was gone except at the higher elevations, and the frost was out of the ground. The sun was warm, but the air was crisp. Everything seemed pretty good — and deceptively peaceful.

There was no sour note until Malone dropped in at the office to talk with Putnam. Wheeler was already gone, and the frowns on the two Putnam faces suggested that there had been something of a scene. Isabel promptly confirmed it. 'I hope you're satisfied,' she greeted Malone, fixing him with an angry stare. 'I don't know why you hated Mark, but you've had your way. He's gone — with nothing whatever proved against him!'

He ignored her tone. 'I was hoping you'd help with the proof,' he said mildly. 'My guess is that Wheeler did more than simply pass along information to Hatfield and the pair who came in ahead of him. I think he might have fouled up a few other things.'

'Such as what?' Putnam demanded.

'Supply inventory. He had a good chance to do it. I think every record ought to be checked against the materials on hand. We can't afford to depend on his records. Imagine what a mess we'd have later on in the summer if it turned out that some of the stuff shown on the books wasn't actually here.'

'You expect me to bolster your ridiculous charges by making such a search?' Isabel demanded.

'Why not? You'll have the time. This office won't be so busy now that the big supply push is about done.'

'You've got a nerve! You know perfectly well that our enemy is this man Hatfield.

Why don't you do something about him and not spend your time trying to turn Mark Wheeler into the villain?'

Malone motioned for Putnam to stay out of it. 'Let's understand each other, Miss Putnam. I fired Wheeler. It was my responsibility. I'm not going to argue the point, and I don't give a thin damn whether or not you find any evidence against him. All I'm concerned about is the chance that maybe he pulled other tricks that might cause us trouble. I'm depending on you to find that trouble before it happens — if it's going to happen.'

'I understand well enough. You hated Mark. You don't care whether he was guilty or not.' She turned to her father as though expecting him to rebuke his partner.

Malone didn't wait for the little man to get entangled. 'If you're so worried about justice for dear old Mark — and I suspect he was trying to be just that — ask our friend Withers about him. I think Mr. Withers will be willing to admit now that it was Wheeler who went snooping through your desk and read that first letter from Hannibal.'

The frail clerk looked unhappy but nodded. 'It wasn't my place to carry tales,' he said defensively. 'When he said right out that nobody went near Miss Isabel's desk I couldn't . . . '

'But Wheeler did go to the desk and read that letter?'

'Yes, sir. I'm sorry I didn't say so sooner. He was my boss, in a way. I didn't know . . . '

Malone let it go at that. He didn't propose to go out of his way to develop friendly relations with Isabel Putnam, but he didn't need to rub salt into the wound. He had made his point. 'One thing we didn't talk about last night,' he said. 'What would be the chances of stirring up a bit of trouble for Burchell and Hatfield? Somehow I don't like just being a target. I'd rather throw a few punches than just stand back and ward off the other man's.'

'You figure a way,' Putnam told him grimly. 'I couldn't do it.'

Malone went out. He wasn't going to accomplish anything with either of the Putnams this morning.

In spite of that small failure, he had no complaints to make about the day. His own duties amounted to exactly nothing. Flannery had made arrangements with one of Guinn's hostlers so that now spying was being handled by the other team. It was important to have some idea of what Hatfield would do next — and what the role of the two new men would be — but there were definite objections to any more open visits to the Muleskinner Hotel, particularly by Malone. Nothing would be gained by an open personal brawl with Hatfield, and there was the ever-present risk that Tillie Atherton might get her memory into gear. She had plenty of reason to remember Jack Kyle — and to hate him. There was not much sense in adding to the ranks of the enemy.

Two days passed, two fine days in which the grade and rails crept steadily up the winding length of Muleskinner

Gulch. Flannery and Terpin were beginning to revise their estimates. At this rate they might cut several days off the working budget.

That night Flannery got a report from his spy. The two newcomers had let it be known that they were Pinkert men. They gave their names as Clint Wren and Nick Owens. They let everyone understand that they were on the trail of a pair of bandits who answered to the descriptions Tucker and Fredericks. There was no mention of the two names, but the descriptions were clear enough. Hatfield was spending a lot of time with the two newcomers, apparently having struck up a friendship with them.

Terpin was inclined to crow when he brought the informtion to Malone. 'We're still buyin' time fer ourselves with the way we handled that dirty business in the gulch, Lefty Hatfield couldn't find out a goddam thing for hisself, he brung in a couple of bastards to do his huntin' fer him. Makin' believe that he don't know 'em ain't foolin' us none. They're up here to make the hunt he didn't want nobody see him makin'.'

'Fine with us,' Malone commented. 'Maybe we'll have a few extra days before they cook up something different. But don't think that these two were brought in just to play hunters. My guess is that Hatfield dreamed up this Pinkerton yarn on the spur of the moment.'

'Could be that yuh're right. Somehow I don't figger that he'd be so damned anxious to locate a couple o' men he must guess have got to be dead. Once a feller's good to him no more, it ain't likely he'd be interested. Only thing is he wants to know what happened. He ain't sure how much we got on him.'

'Meanwhile, we're making progress.'

'Got any idea what these new jiggers are up to?'

'No. I remember the bandy-legged fellow. At least I've seen him before. He was either a surveyor or some kind of helper with the Kansas Pacific. I don't remember that I ever heard his name.'

'Surveyor, hey? Could it be that they'll

check on our line and mebbe try to tie us up with a lawsuit, claimin' that we're on somebody's land with our rail?'

Malone shook his head. 'It's not likely. I never heard that anybody owned anything in these mountains. No homestead tracts. No Spanish grants this far north. Not even any mining claims near our right-of-way.'

'I'll tell yuh one thing,' Terpin growled. 'We won't be too much longer in findin' out. Makin' believe to be a Pinkerton is kind of a risky deal. The Pinkies don't like havin' no fakes claimin' to be their men. These bastards have got to move fast before they have real Pinks on their necks.'

Suddenly he looked solemn. 'Yuh don't think they're real Pinks, do yuh?'

Malone laughed. 'Afraid your evil past might catch up with you? Don't worry. I'll give you odds that they're not anything but a couple of dollar-hungry lads who have agreed to do a dirty job for Hatfield and Burchell. I think they came in here for some particular purpose but that Hatfield saw his chance to use them for the snooping he didn't want to do himself. I hope they keep on playing Pinkertons for a while. That's so much extra time without more real trouble.'

'Mebbe they'll offer a reward fer them missin' polecats,' Terpin said hopefully. 'Alive or dead? That might let us show 'em some corpses. We could pick up a bit o' enemy money.'

'You've already got some,' Malone reminded him.

The fat man grinned and then sobered. 'Why ain't that a point fer our side to think about? This here's turnin' out to be a money fight. We're in trouble because we ain't got enough. Mebbe we could do somethin' that would make this Burchell bastard come up a mite short, too.'

Malone laughed. 'What now? Are you planning to rob the Mountain Bank?'

'Don't gimme ideas. That's one kind o' crooked work I never tried. Mebbe I been missin' a trick.'

Two more days passed in which the grade and track men shoved iron well up toward the long cliff. Malone took time each morning to make certain that the team of Hatfield, Wren, and Owens hadn't started any new campaign. In the afternoons he made it a point to be on hand when the train arrived, watching for strangers who might be enemy reinforcements. Outside these two small efforts, he spent a lot of time acting as Hannibal Putnam's legman. Somewhat to his own surprise, he liked it. He was doing something constructive, helping to get the line built. Maybe what he was doing wasn't really as important as the protective duties that he had to be ready to perform, but at least he was taking a hand in actual building, not just standing around with a gun while other men did the work.

He discovered that he could go in and out of the office without wrangling with Isabel. Neither of them mentioned Wheeler. They both knew that the man had slipped away on the day following his discharge, going down with the empty rail cars. It wasn't likely that he would be back. His role in this affair had been like Grimes's. Both men had been useful to Burchell in the early stages of the little war, but neither of them had anything to offer now. Petty delays and minor troubles would not satisfy Burchell's needs now. Only a major effort could stop the rapid progress of Terpin's crews. Malone realized it and determined he would be ready.

The fake Pinkertons began to stir. There was nothing secret about it. Malone heard the story even before Flannery's spy reported. The supposed detectives announced that they were convinced that the men they were trailing were the murderers of the two S. & F. teamsters. They had quite a yarn worked out. According to the statement they made at the Muleskinner bar, they believed that the fugitive bandits, using the names of Tucker and Fredericks, had hung around Muleskinner until they were afraid their pursuers would catch up with them. Then they had ridden back into the mountains, probably intending to hole up somewhere around the mining camps. It happened that they had met the powder wagon that the railroad was sending up the trail, and one of the railroad teamsters had recognized them. They had killed both wagoners to prevent any report going out about them. Then they must have gone on about their business of losing themselves in the neighborhood of Silverdale.

'Yuh got to hand it to 'em,' Terpin conceded when he discussed the report with Malone. 'They sure as hell tied up a lot of loose ends in their lie. Kinda got to admire smart liars like that pair.'

'Not so smart,' Malone retorted. 'Did you ever hear of a couple of lawmen telling everybody what they were planning to do and why? For real detectives to set out on a man hunt with all this gabbiness would be like hunting game with a brass band.'

'Hell, Lefty, yuh're spoilin' it fer me. I was just gettin' around to likin' the bastards fer their sneakiness.'

'Make up your mind. A few days ago

you were yearning to be a bank robber. Now you're cheering for the sneaky type of thing. Your criminal instincts are getting all mixed up.'

'I been honest fer quite a spell now,' Terpin told him loftily. 'Could be I'm a mite confused at myself. Mebbe I could figger out a way to get it all put together somehow.'

'You'd better spend your time figuring out how you're going to keep in touch with me. When those polecats move, I've got to keep an eye on 'em. I want to know what they're really planning to do. Could be a bit difficult.'

S. & F. men returning from evening visits to the Muleskinner reported that the bogus Pinkertons and Hatfield were making preparations for some kind of trip. Guinn had rented horses to the newcomers, and Hatfield already had one, bought previous to his earlier trips up the gulch. All three were stocking up with supplies, which hinted at a journey of some distance.

Malone took the hint. When daylight

came he was at the point where the graders would begin to work that day, watching the wagon trail from his higher elevation. He didn't think that the trio would have left before daylight; their public planning didn't suggest that they were going to do anything secret. Not at first.

When the little engine pushed its load of men and materials up the grade, they still had not appeared. Terpin came along to pass the word that they were moving, that they had left the Muleskinner Hotel just as the train started. 'Ain't makin' no try at hidin' their moves,' he told Malone. 'So yuh got to be ready fer somethin' real sneaky. Looks like they're tryin' to throw us off guard.'

'I'll keep shady,' Malone promised.

It wasn't difficult to keep the three men in sight when they finally showed up below the new railroad line. Malone had ridden ahead into the timber, halting at spots where he could see the wagon tracks below. It became pretty dull.

Then he had a chance to watch

some interesting gestures. The men he was watching halted at the spot where the ambush had taken place. Hatfield seemed to be explaining what he knew, the waving of his arms indicating the spot where the wagoners had been killed and the direction from which the gunfire was supposed to have come. That much was known to anyone who had bothered to listen to reports. It was no secret that the two men had been ambushed at this point.

Then Hatfield's explanation began to take on a little more interest for the watcher above him. He pointed up on the mountain and then ahead at the line of cliffs. Malone had to do some guessing, but there was no doubt in his mind that Hatfield was describing the roundabout path by which Tucker and Fredericks had reached the ambush point. It also seemed pretty clear that he was explaining the blasting plan that had gone awry. If there had been any doubt as to Hatfield's knowledge of the murder plan, it would have ended right here. His motions made it clear that he knew exactly what the missing men had planned to do.

For Malone, it was an unnecessary warning along another line. Hatfield wouldn't be talking like this unless he trusted the men with him. It meant that the new operators were just as ruthless as the other pair had been.

The men below circled the area for several minutes, studying the brush on both sides of the trail. Malone watched with some amusement. Hatfield had already looked for sign here. Now that extra days had passed, there wasn't much chance that these men would find anything. Not unless bears or wolves or some other predators had dug up the dead men. It wasn't a pretty thought.

An hour later they gave up on the job and began to ride on past the cliff. Malone took pains to keep them in view constantly. Now that Hatfield had shown himself to be eloquent with gestures, it seemed like good sense to watch the man. Maybe he would betray himself.

Still nothing happened. They rode past the base of the cliff without seeming to pay any particular attention to it. When they struck the steep climb, they pulled aside to let some wagons pass but made no attempt to ride back into the timber. Malone had a little more difficulty keeping an eye on them now. He could no longer follow the railroad's survey line because this was the stretch where the rails made their big loop to gain altitude. He had to work his way through heavy timber on the slope, only seeing the three men at intervals. But there was nothing to hint that they had done anything but ride in the periods when he could not watch them.

They went through the pass at a casual gait, stopping twice to talk with wagoners out of Silverdale. Probably asking about the men they pretended to be following, Malone thought. There had to be some significance to the fuss they were making about the search. They wanted everybody to know that they were on the trail of outlaws. Consequently it was important to keep a wary eye out for whatever real purpose was being concealed behind the talk.

They pulled aside to make the climb up to O'Boyle's camp. Malone kept his distance, watching while they spent nearly an hour at the camp itself, making no attempt to ride out along the line where the men were working. Malone was getting more puzzled by the minute, but he took time to see that O'Boyle's gang was making as rapid progress as the larger crew at the other end of the gulch. Hatfield and his men could see what was happening. They would know that their next move had to be made without much delay.

When the three riders headed on down the trail to the mining camps, which collectively had been named Silverdale, Malone did not follow. He didn't believe that they could come up with much mischief in that quarter. Better to check with O'Boyle's men and find out what sort of tack Hatfield had been taking with his questions.

There wasn't much to learn. The two

'detectives' had given out the same story as at Muleskinner. They had asked if anyone had seen two men of the descriptions of Tucker and Fredericks. Then they had added a question: 'Has anyone seen a couple of horses bearing Double S brands?'

They had not pushed very hard with any of the questions, O'Boyle's wrangler reported, his grin a little wider than necessary. Malone didn't ask for explanations. He had seen the two horses with 88's on their shoulders, and he felt certain that they were the animals that had been brought up to the grade camp after the gulch fight. He wondered whether Hatfield had seen them. It seemed likely. Jim Hatfield knew enough about thievery of all types so that he would not miss a simple case of brand-blotting, particularly when he was already suspicious.

Malone remained overnight at the camp, passing on the latest information to O'Boyle. Mostly it was a matter of explaining the things Putnam had discussed on the evening of his arrival.

O'Boyle was entitled to know. He had as big a stake in the enterprise as Flannery.

Next morning Malone moved on, scouting rather than trying to reach Silverdale. And that was rather an odd feature, he thought. He was a partner in the mines, but he had never even seen them. Somehow he wasn't very curious. Plenty of time to take a look when the railroad was turning Silverdale into a going concern.

In the middle of the morning, he was glad that he had moved with caution. Hatfield and his cronies were coming back. Probably they had spent the evening putting on their act. Now they would get down to business, having established their supposed errand in the mountains. Malone took to the timber and began trailing them once more.

He kept a close watch on them as they backtracked. This time they didn't turn aside to the grade camp but followed the wagon tracks straight up into the pass. Then they changed their tactics. Instead of following the gulch trail, they turned aside and began to ride along the line of the railroad's survey, taking the wide loop where the tracks would leave the gulch. Malone closed in just a little. Now he was going to see what this elaborate fake was all about.

11

It was a little past noon when Malone had to pull back in a hurry. He had caught a glimpse of a rider corning back toward him, and presently he saw that it was Hatfield. Fortunately he had ducked away from the survey line some minutes earlier, and it was fairly easy for him to find a thicket where he could take cover, far enough up on the mountain so that the movements of his horse would not be heard above the sound of wind in the pines.

It was a tense moment. Hatfield either was suspicious or was taking extra precautions. His movements were guarded, careful. Every few yards, he pulled up and listened. Evidently he expected that someone was trailing him.

Malone spent an anxious twenty minutes while he watched the lanky gun hawk carefully studying the ground along his own back trail. If he went far enough back toward the pass, he would be certain to find Malone's tracks.

But he didn't go that far. He missed by what Malone estimated was mere yards. After pausing as though to listen once more, he swung his horse to ride toward his companions at a rapid pace. Malone waited until he was sure that Hatfield's scouting trip was really completed, then eased down the slope until he could get a good look at the brushed-out strip where the surveyors had worked. Now he led his horse, picking a way along a ledge that ran almost parallel to the line that was to carry S. & F. rails.

Finally he saw them. Hatfield had caught up with the pair, and the three of them were walking around, looking at the S. & F. survey stakes and doing a bit more of the gesticulating that Malone was learning to interpret. It was clear that they were discussing the line and the way it had been laid out to gain altitude. He left his horse and started down the mountain on foot, working cautiously as he tried to get close enough to see what they were doing. It took quite a while to find a spot where he could see without exposing himself, and he was much too far away to hear any of the words passing between them.

What was important was that they had set up a transit, evidently a compact sort of instrument that could be carried in saddlebags and a slicker roll. Owens — apparently the bandy-legged man was using that name — seemed to be giving the orders. He waved his partner up along the line of the S. & F. stakes, sighting carefully and making notations. Hatfield took no part in the operation but stood back with one arm hooked over his saddle horn as he watched.

It was well along toward evening when they finished what they were doing, and Malone still couldn't see the point of it. To all intents and purposes, they were simply checking the accuracy of the S. & F. survey. It didn't make much sense.

When they prepared to make camp for the night, he knew that he had to take a chance. There was no way to get an idea of their plans except by eavesdropping. Maybe a surveyor could have guessed without hearing the talk that went with the operation, but Malone was not a surveyor. He'd done a little work with survey gangs, mostly lending a volunteer hand for a few minutes at a time, but he understood what was happening only in a general way.

When a small fire was going and the trio were making a real greenhorn supper, with plenty of canned goods, Malone began to work his way down to listening range. He didn't mind the smell of their food too much. It was worth going hungry to feel that he was keeping his job under control. The first bit of delay had gained a lot of valuable ground. Now it appeared that Hatfield was cooking up another scheme that might be made to backfire. Possibly this defensive campaign was exactly the right thing for S. & F. Simply stopping the Burchell-Hatfield efforts was an excellent time-buyer. The important thing was to do the stopping in a manner that would confuse the enemy. Every day that the opposition spent in hesitation was a day in which the work crews could make progress. It wasn't a very spectacular way to fight a war, but it was proving effective — and it didn't require Lefty Malone to act like Jack Kyle.

The tedious crawl toward the camp-fire turned out to be a lot of work for practically nothing. By the time Malone was within earshot of the camp, the three men were rolling into their blankets for the night, obviously worn out from so much riding. At least their talk seemed to have only that one topic.

Then Hatfield asked, 'Yuh sure yuh got that angle figured right? It's got to be just like I told yuh.'

The bandy-legged man's reply was sleepily irritable. 'I told you nobody's going to spot it! Why in hell did you bring me in on this job if you can't take my word for things?'

'I just want to make sure. We can't afford any more mistakes. In the mornin' I'll swing another loop around here and make sure that nobody's trailed us. Then you boys git to work. Do this hunk of it first. Then we'll try to find the other place they told me about.'

That was the end of it for Malone. He crept away as silently as he had come, taking a lot more time to get back to his horse because he had to find his way in the dark and make no sound. The night had come down still and cold, no wind stirring to cover his movements.

He thought about what he had heard, but he couldn't make much sense out of it. Something was about to happen, and he knew that he had to find out what it was. He had been given ample warning that in the morning he would have to stay clear of Hatfield's scouting trip, but he didn't think he would have any trouble.

He wondered if Mark Wheeler had supplied the information that Hatfield seemed to have about the line. Evidently the enemy was interested in two spots that they had known about in advance. One spot had already been checked.

The other had not yet been identified by them, simply mentioned in a manner that made it clear that they knew what they were looking for.

Out of his perplexity, Malone could find just one ray of comfort. The new move on the part of the enemy was consuming time. Another day or two had already been gained. Maybe a bit more could be squeezed out.

He ate sparingly of hard rations at dawn, then moved his horse to a spot higher on the mountain and picked a look-out spot that permitted him a fair view of the lower slopes. He saw Hatfield only at intervals, but he could guess at the pattern the man was riding. When he was sure that the scout job was done, he moved down the slope once more, this time leaving his horse behind him.

It took time, but eventually he was in position to see Hatfield again watching the two men at work. They had their transit set up once more and were surveying a line of their own, a line that seemed to run along a ledge just below the line that the S. & F. engineers had laid out.

Malone wished that he knew more about surveying, but he was beginning to get the general idea even before he saw something that gave him all the hint he needed. Owens and Wren were not using their own stakes to mark out the line they were running; they were pulling up S. & F. stakes and removing them to the new line.

Now it began to make sense. At this point the railroad would be making its gradual climb to the pass. Several wide loops were planned so that no part of the grade would be too steep. The key to mountain railroading was a proper grade, Malone knew. Now that gradient was being altered, carefully and by men who seemed to know what they were doing.

He let the idea knock around in his mind. This was a stretch where Flannery's gang would do the work. They would come to the point where the stakes had been moved and would start grading a wrong line. It probably would look all right to them because it seemed to follow a natural ledge. They would hurry along — as they were doing, everyone working at top speed — and would have a roadbed with rails on it stretching out in the wrong direction before they realized what had happened.

The rest of the picture didn't come clear. Malone could guess that sooner or later somebody would wake up, but not before there had been days, maybe as much as a week, of lost effort. Then there would be more loss of time in taking up the track and moving it to the proper grade. Or maybe nobody would find out what had happened until they found themselves building track on a grade that a steam engine couldn't handle. Obviously that was the way it would work out if the false line continued. Not gaining enough altitude along this stretch would mean an impossible grade farther along in order to reach the pass.

He considered what he ought to do now. A small demonstration would quickly break up the operation, of course.

Everything depended on the job being done in secrecy so that the construction crews would be fooled. Simply letting Hatfield and his men know that they were under surveillance would break it up.

But that didn't seem like much of an idea. They would only try something else, maybe something violent. Perhaps something could be gained by a cat-and-mouse game. There would not be too much difficulty in restaking the proper line; the marks of the old stakes would still be fairly obvious even though the survey crews hadn't brushed out the line here as cleanly as they had done along the walls of Muleskinner Gulch. Meanwhile, a waiting game would buy time. That was all that really mattered.

He watched the men run their line for a good half mile. Then they simply quit, blocked by a vertical wall of rock that had the real line at its top. Malone had to grin at the thought of what Terpin would say if he found his grading crews running into this solid barrier. A small grin wasn't out of place now that the danger was known.

He had to pull back then. The sabotage party was getting ready to move, apparently to the 'other spot' that Hatfield had mentioned. Evidently they had been advised of two places along the line where terrain made it possible to fool grading crews. Probably they didn't figure to fool the construction men twice, but at least they would have two chances of doing it. Even one false move would wreck a tight schedule.

Malone resumed the tedious business of trailing his men. They rode across country this time, cutting off one of the big loops and emerging on the survey line between the big cliff and the first long bend. It was midafternoon by the time they located the place they were seeking, and the previous performance was repeated. Hatfield rode a circle around the area to protect against observation. Malone dodged him and went back to see how the two surveyors were studying their problem. The situation seemed to be very much the same. There was a natural ledge that looked perfect for a rail line but had been avoided by the S. & F. surveyors. Malone guessed that this one climbed a little too much instead of not enough, but the technical part of it wasn't important. Now he knew what was intended.

He decided that there was no point in trying to work out countermeasures by himself. Better to let Terpin know what was happening. Maybe the fat man could come up with an idea.

Soon Hatfield rode away, apparently heading for Muleskinner Gulch and the trail back to the wagon depot. Malone followed. There was not much point in sticking around to see what the surveyors were going to do next morning; he already was pretty sure about that point. He had to know what Hatfield was doing and where he was located before he could bring Terpin in on any defensive move. Maybe Hatfield even had another plan ready to put into operation. It seemed likely; the men who planned to take over this railroad line and make a profit out of it wouldn't want to wreck it any more than necessary. Even the plan to blast the long cliff wouldn't have resulted in major damage but only in the delay of hacking out a new line. It was a point to be considered.

He followed Hatfield long enough to feel sure that the gunman was really on his way to Muleskinner by way of the wagon trail. Then he aimed for the cliff line where he expected that Flannery's crew would now be working. If they had maintained their pace, they would have track all along the tops of the bluffs by this time.

He swung in at the north end of the cliffs, a little disappointed when he did not find the grade line already there. Nor could he hear any sounds to indicate that the engine was around the bend. Now that the men were working so far away from their quarters, they rode in both directions, the engine coming up to get them after making the daily trip out to Fremont Junction.

It wasn't until he rounded the first

real bend of the line that he saw what had happened. A big chunk of the rock face had cracked loose and had tumbled down the side of the gorge, almost blocking the wagon trail below, This was what Tucker and Fredericks had been trying to accomplish on a larger scale. For a moment Malone blamed himself for not guarding against a second attempt at this vital spot, but then he decided that there had been no blasting involved. A portion of the cliff had simply proved to be unstable. Probably a natural split had opened up as soon as the graders began to work there. He hoped there hadn't been any deaths or injuries when the cliff broke away. Losing men was bad, not only for the poor devils who were killed but for the company and its prospects. Other workmen began to lose a bit of their zeal when a bad accident occurred.

He found that he could get around the break. Already there had been some tentative grading done, and he assumed that Terpin was probing at the gulch slope, trying to decide whether to bridge the gap or cut the whole line farther back into the mountain. One way or another, this was a major disaster. Everything was going to be held up for at least a couple of weeks.

It was ticklish business getting his horse around the cave-in area with darkness coming on, but finally he was safely on the far side. Then he could see that a decision had been made. Digging had already been started so that the track could be tucked a little deeper into the mountain. That meant that a few hundred yards of the rail that was already in place would have to be moved. A lot more dirt and rock would have to be taken out before that could happen — and the digging job up ahead was going to be far more trouble than had been anticipated. Bad luck had done what Hatfield and his thugs had failed to do.

When he finally rode into Muleskinner, well after dark, Malone learned that the rock slide had not been the only bit of ill fortune. The second-hand locomotive had burned out a couple of tubes and was being repaired with the materials available, the horse-shoer doing the work.

'We'll be usin' wagons fer a week at least,' Terpin told him. 'If Abe kin git the old teakettle runnin' well enough so's we kin take her down to the D. & R. G. shops, it'll still take near a week to git her fixed up. Right now we don't know but what we'll have to hire a Rio Grande engine to come up and haul her down. And we ain't sure they'll do the job on credit, which is about the only way we kin git done.'

'What about that rock slide?' Malone asked. 'Do you think there was any monkey business there?'

'Nope. It jest happened. Anyway, it was a good thing the damned rock didn't hold up fer a spell and then decide to rip itself loose when we had a train goin' over it. Not that there's much cheer in that kind o' thinkin'. Now we got to probe fer more flaws in the rock and dig in a mite deeper so's we don't have to depend on that damned edge bein' solid.'

'What does all this do to our schedule?'

'Hard to tell, dammit! It's goin' to make a good week of extra work gradin' along the cliff top. Or it would take week if we could keep on the way we was goin'. Without that damned engine to haul stuff up the grade, we'll have to put men to work haulin' with teams. That slows every damned thing down so's I can't even guess what this is goin' to cost us. Three weeks, mebbe.'

'We've still got a little elbow room. Flannery predicted that we'd get a train over the line by the third week of June. Figure a three-week delay, and we're still in business by mid-July. Still two weeks to the good on Old Put's deadline.'

Terpin shook his head. 'Flannery was talkin' to make the old man feel good. We wouldn't ha' put a train over the line before early July. Now we're goin' to have to hump ourselves to make the August first date — and we can't afford no bad weather, no accidents, no nothin'. If that damned engine don't git fixed, we ain't goin' to make it nohow.'

Malone hated to add to the fat man's woe, but he related what he had seen in the mountains. 'I want you to take a look at it. They haven't done any damage, I hope. Nothing we can't fix in a hurry.'

Terpin stared. 'Yuh mean to tell me yuh watched them bastards foulin' up our survey line and yuh didn't do nothin' about it? What the hell, Lefty! Yuh had yer chance to gun 'em all down. They deserved it — and we'd be clear o' the goddam skunks.'

'Maybe I was wrong. I figured to play for time. The other case worked out pretty good that way.'

'Hell! It makes me laugh when I remember that day I got to thinkin' that yuh might be Jack Kyle. That sonofabitch wouldn't sit back on his butt and let a couple o' ornery bastards pull a stunt like that!'

Malone didn't let himself sound annoyed. He simply asked, 'Want to go out with me in the morning and get a look at their work? You'll know what has to be done about it. Maybe you'll even get a bright idea about handling the men doing the job. Remember, we're still trying to buy time. Now we need it worse than ever.'

'Yuh're damned right I'll go. But I don't figure we're buyin' time no more. We're fightin' fer it!' He turned away in supreme disgust but looked back to ask, 'What happened to Hatfield?'

'I think he headed back here. You'd better check with that man Flannery keeps on duty as a spy.'

'Not that it'll mean nothin'. Yuh shoulda shot the bastard when yuh had the chance. Have yuh told the old man about this?'

'No. I didn't figure to visit the office. They've got enough trouble.'

This time Terpin went off. His language made it very clear that he didn't think much of Lefty Malone and it didn't make a bit of difference whether or not Malone was his boss.

12

Luckily for Malone, the cook didn't seem to share Terpin's low opinion of him. A late supper was supplied, and the man was almost genial when Malone asked for a pail of hot water. Maybe the cook's good nature was partly a reflection of the fact that Malone had lost his grim scowl during the meal and was smiling to himself when he asked for the hot water. Even a camp cook can take pride in an obviously satisfied customer.

It would have been a letdown for the fellow to have learned that his late visitor scarcely knew what he had been eating. The smile was due partly to anticipation and partly to a wry feeling that what he was about to do was the kind of sneaky trick that Terpin would enjoy.

A shave and what passed for a bath made him feel even better. Being clean generally helped and the shave was a necessity. He didn't propose to let Tillie

Atherton see him behind even a faint scrub of whiskers. The clean shave was practically a disguise now.

The Muleskinner bar was doing a brisk business when he eased through the open doorway and took a quick look around. With supper long since over, the tables were occupied by poker playes and several groups of wagoners who laughed or argued over their drinks. It occurred to Malone that Brian Guinn had a good thing going. The peppery little invalid hired men to drive his teams and then took back a good portion of their wages by selling them liquor.

One sweeping glance gave him the location of the three people who interested him most. Guinn was behind the bar, helping his two bartenders in what seemed to be a rush of business. Tillie was making herself as attractive as possible to a stout man who looked as though he might be a salesman of some sort. Hatfield was at a table with the black bearded man Malone had seen on his earlier visit. Malone was reminded that he didn't know where the bearded man fitted into the picture. Maybe he was only Hatfield's agent among the teamsters, but it was worth a little effort to get the truth. Maybe Flannery's man could find out about the fellow.

He saw that Hatfield had recognized him. The tall gunnie undoubtedly knew that the railroad's Lefty Malone was the same whiskery gent who had humiliated him in this same room. Maybe he knew — without being certain — that Malone had been active in a few other areas. There was a long moment in which the two men exchanged stares, Malone wondering whether Hatfield would try something. The moment of danger seemed to pass, and Malone went across to where Guinn was finishing up the last batch of orders.

The little man looked twice before he realized who was in front of him. Then he said worriedly, 'You're not going to make trouble, I hope.'

'I don't make it,' Malone told him. 'I try to avoid it. That's why I'm here.' It was at least partly true.

'Funny way to duck trouble, comin' here.' He nodded toward Hatfield. 'He ain't forgot you, mister.'

'Any place we can talk? This is business.'

Guinn looked to see that the two bartenders had things under control, then motioned toward a vacant table in a corner. 'Over there. I'd ask you to check your gun, but I see Hatfield's wearin' his. Seems like he thinks he makes the rules in here.'

'I don't figure there'll be gun-play,' Malone assured him.

Guinn let a smile creep partly across his thin lips. 'Seems like you managed real good without one last time.'

Malone didn't know whether the little man was referring to the brief scuffle with Hatfield in the hotel or whether he had some idea about what had happened later. Maybe it was a little of both. It wouldn't have taken too much shrewd guessing to have figured out the other part. 'Like I said,' Malone repeated, 'I'm not here to make trouble. We've already got trouble. You're in it because you've got a deal with the troublemakers.'

'Prove it or don't make claims.'

Malone shook his head. 'The proofs not the kind that would hold up in court, either in a criminal case or in a breach-of-contract suit. You'll have to decide for yourself whether I'm telling it straight.'

He outlined the whole situation, filling in details where possible and omitting only the part about disposing of the bodies of Tucker and Fredericks. He thought that Guinn got the point and could make a pretty sharp guess about what had actually happened out there in the gulch.

One outright lie completed the tale, 'We expected to be cramped by not getting the line built on time — which is what these scoundrels were trying for. Now we're in the clear. Refinancing is all set. They can't take over an unfinished line, but they don't know it. They can still hurt us, of course, but they'll hurt theselves at the same time. If we tell them that their game won't work, they won't believe us — naturally enough. So I figure that the way to start getting rid of them is to take away the toe-hold they got by making their deal with you.'

'Why should I pull your chestnuts out of the fire?'

'Because they're your chestnuts, too. The outfit that took the option on your company never planned to go through with the deal. All they wanted was a good reason to be up here raising hell. Maybe it also helped that a wagon outfit would have some reason to want the rails stopped. At least it made their reasons a little foggy at first. Now we know who we're bucking and we know why. We know they can't win — but they don't know it. What we want is to get them out of here legally before they cause any more senseless trouble. We know that you want to sell out but that you'd like to pick up the profit that this season will bring. So we'll offer you a deal. We buy your whole outfit at a price to be set when the agreement becomes a contract, delivery to be made by you at any date you choose between now and the end of this year. That should be about what you want, I think.'

Guinn nodded with undisguised interest. 'You mean you'd take an option on the whole setup, leaving time of delivery to me?'

'Right. I said any time between now and the end of the year. If you prefer, we'll postpone that date a little. Just in case we don't get all finished with the rail line this season, we wouldn't mind if you stayed on here through next spring.'

The little man shook his head. 'Not necessary. This summer is the finish for me in these mountains. I'm heading for Arizona.'

'Suit yourself. What we have to know is whether your contract with Hatfield and Burchell will interfere with the deal we're offering.'

'Burchell? Who's he?'

'Hatfield's partner. I forgot that he was keeping under cover. Do they have you tied up, or can you get out of the arrangement you've made with them?'

Guinn started to reply but changed to a whisper immediately. 'Careful. Hatfield's on his way over here. Got the wind up, I'd say.'

'Good.' Malone nodded. 'We'll try to remember that this is all strictly business. I hope'

The tall gunman approached warily but with a scowl that warned that he intended to find out what this talk was all about. Malone took some of the bite out of him when he waved him casually to an empty chair.

'Might as well sit down and hear this, Hatfield,' he invited. 'No fancy talk. No bluster. You know who I am. I know who you are. I know what you're trying to do and what you already did. Right?'

'Meaning what?' Hatfield sneered, still standing.

'Sit down. You don't have to be ready to grab a gun. Shooting won't fix anything.'

'I wasn't . . . ' He clamped his lean jaw tight and took the chair.

Malone nodded calmly. 'So it's this way. You and Burchell want to bust up construction so you can grab this railroad. Let's don't argue about the details. Maybe I know more about them than you do. If Burchell's fixing to double-cross you in any way, I wouldn't want to spill anything that would keep him from doing it.' He was being very casual about it now, enjoying the moment because it was so clear that Hatfield was worried. 'I just made Mr. Guinn an offer for his holdings here. I think he was just about to give me an answer. Maybe it's just as well that you hear it.'

That put Guinn on the spot, but the little man didn't hesitate. 'I want to sell out,' he said slowly. 'But I can afford to wait for the right price. As it stands right now, Hatfield has an option to buy. The option's up in a little over two weeks. No point in making my position sound complicated. I'll honor the option if it's picked up. If it lapses, I'm in the market. Want to talk price?'

Malone shook his head. 'Not now. You

don't have anything to sell.'

'And you people don't have anything to buy with!' Hatfield snapped.

'Don't depend on it. There's always somebody who's willing to get in on a good thing.'

'Who?'

'That's none of your business. As a matter of fact, I didn't need to tell you this much. You were so damned insistent on busting in on this talk that I thought you might as well know that your crooked plans won't work.'

Hatfield started to kick back his chair. 'Crooked plans!' he exclaimed in pretended outrage. 'We ain't . . .'

'Save the gab. You've pulled every crooked little trick in the book to keep this line from going through. You brought that slug Grimes in to talk up a fake Indian threat. You tried to hire men away from the S. & F. after Grimes had scared them. You sent a couple of murderers out to blow up a piece of roadbed. You had some of our materials sent off to wrong places. I'm not even sure that you didn't have a hand in having our one engine go bust at the wrong time.' He wasn't trying to make the final accusation sound too serious. The main idea was to avoid mentioning the job now being done by Hatfield's surveyors in the mountains. Maybe it was just as well to let the man think that this bit of trickery was still on the possible list. 'I'm tellin' you now, mister, you might as well give up and go back to Burchell. Maybe next time you'll find easier meat.'

Hatfield looked ready to go for his gun. He turned red as Malone laid it on, then the red faded and all expression left his face. Guinn sensed the danger and stepped directly between the two men, placing his frail body squarely across the table. 'That's all!' he snapped. 'I've got no part in this fight — and I don't intend to have you using my place for it!'

'Suits me,' Malone told him. 'I just put my cards on the table.'

Hatfield didn't say a word. He stood up slowly, scowling at Malone. Then he wheeled and headed across the room toward a far door, not even speaking to the black-bearded man.

Malone grinned wryly at Guinn. 'Any windows over that way that cover the front? I don't want to get a slug in my back when I go out.'

* * *

Terpin was awake when Malone got back to his bunk in the warehouse. The fat man was still grumbling.

'What the hell yuh been doin' now? Out playin' games with the varmints yuh shoulda killed?'

'Something like that,' Malone replied. 'And don't yell so damned loud. You'll wake up men who've got a hard day's work ahead of them.'

'Yuh better not be pullin' nothin', Malone,' the fat man warned. 'Like I told yuh first off when yuh showed up here, I got a stake in this thing and I aim to make it good.'

'So listen and stop blowing off steam.' He outlined what had happened at the hotel, with Terpin's grumbling getting louder with almost every sentence. Finally Malone gave him a chance to say something.

'What in hell was the idea of all that goddam foolishness? We ain't got no money to buy up a passel o' jackasses and wagons. We ain't got . . .'

'Of course we haven't. But do you think Hatfield and his partner are going to take the chance that we might do it?'

'So they pick up the option and buy Guinn out. How in hell does that do us any good?'

'I haven't got that part figured out exactly. The idea didn't come to me until I was eating supper. Then I . . .'

'Hell of an idea! Now we kin git sued fer breach o' contract as well as losin' the railroad.'

'No contract yet. I don't think there will be. I'm gambling that the enemy makes a buy.'

'I still don't see . . .'

'I'm trying to tell you. Up to now we've been the ones who've been hard up for cash. Now we put the squeeze on the opposition.'

'But . . .'

'Figure out what Guinn's going to ask for his outfit. There's quite an investment there. Now consider where Burchell is going to dig up the cash. He must be running mighty close after buying up those S. & F. bonds. A bank can afford just so much frozen assets and then they've got trouble. I'm working on the idea that it wouldn't hurt any to let people in Denver get the word that the Mountain Bank is loaded up with the bonds of a railroad company that might never get built and that they've just bought a freight outfit that is on the point of losing their line. The two things don't go together, I know, but most people won't realize that.'

Terpin's expression changed slowly. Finally he was grinning broadly. 'Kinda figurin' to git even fer the Ute talk, hey? Burn 'em with their own kind o' fire.'

'Something like that. We can talk about it while we do something about those two jiggers in the mountains. The details shouldn't be too hard.'

'I take back what I said about yuh, Lefty. Yuh're almost as sneaky as me.'

'Thanks. Now I can sleep.'

'Don't git so damned smart. I reckon yuh heard about the yarn that Hatfield's tellin' since he got back. Accordin' to him, them Pinkertons are chasin' their bandits clean across the mountains. Don't sound like he expects his polecats to come back through here.'

'That part I forgot,' Malone admitted. 'We'll keep our eyes skinned when we ride out tomorrow. I think I fooled him into believing that we haven't tumbled to this trick, but there's a chance that he might want to make sure.'

They rode out ahead of the work crews in the gray of a cold dawn, two burly workmen who answered to the names of Lafe and Jiggers going along with them. Lafe carried a Winchester, but Jiggers wore a six-gun as though he knew what it was for. Both of them had been let in on the secret and were clearly anticipating something a little more exciting than laying rails. Malone had a feeling that a couple of crooked surveyors were going to have a bad time.

They delayed briefly at a spot where the new rail line gave them a good view of the wagon trail. There was no sign of Hatfield. It had been agreed that Flannery would send a man out to pass the word if Hatfield made a move toward the pass, so they didn't waste much time there. Terpin was itching to get on with the job ahead of them.

When they reached the spot where Malone had last seen the surveyors in action, the country was bare of trespassers. Lafe and Jiggers went out to scout around for a short distance, while Malone showed Terpin the stretch where the stakes had been moved. The fat man said nothing for a good ten minutes. He squinted along both lines, tracing the old one by the signs of brush-cutting and by the stake holes, which they could still find easily enough. He was no mere loudmouth now; he was studying grades with the eye of a man who knew his business.

'Real booby trap, goddammit!' he said finally. 'Falls below the real grade jest barely so's it wouldn't hardly git noticed. If Flannery had his gang workin' under pressure — like they sure as hell would be — they'd run their line right down where them stakes show 'em. Three-four days' work wasted on line that'd have to be all ripped up again. Let's see how far they done it.'

The false line had been run for nearly a quarter of a mile. It simply ended where a rocky projection broke out of the slope. Maybe the tricksters had hoped that the construction crew would waste time in a long blasting job before they discovered their mistake. Even without that extra problem, the disastrous results were easy to foresee.

Lafe came back to report that they'd found the trail of two riders heading toward the pass. Now it was clear why Hatfield had reported that the men were going in another direction. For some reason they did not plan to return to

Muleskinner.

Malone led the way once more. They stopped at the stretch where he had first seen the false staking being done. This time Terpin spent less time in looking it over. The idea was exactly the same. Flannery would have had two chances to make a mistake.

After that the trail of the two surveyors led straight into the pass. Apparently they were going to hole up at Silverdale until any chances of trouble had passed. Or perhaps there was more to the scheme and they would stick around to handle it. Terpin was grumbling again, blaming Malone for not doing something when he had the chance.

They came out of the north end of the pass where the wagon trail and the survey line separated. The sign they were following took the survey line.

'Mighta knowed it!' Terpin exclaimed. 'They're fixin' to set up a trap fer O'Boyle. If they'd git both of our gangs to wastin' time, we'd sure enough be licked.'

Malone nodded. 'This time I don't

know where to look for them. You know the grades. Figure out where they could pull that stunt of theirs.'

'I got it all worked out,' Terpin told him. 'Let's git movin'. Mebbe we'll ketch the bastards right in the act.'

'Catch 'em,' Malone agreed. 'Don't shoot 'em. Better to make 'em go back and replace all the stakes.'

Terpin guffawed. 'Lefty, I take it all back — again. Yuh got the damnedest ideas!'

13

Terpin thought about it as they moved down along the grade north of the pass. Finally he made a decision. 'Looks to me like them bastards know their business. Both places back there they picked spots where it looked like a choice of lines. If they scouted this side as good as they done the other, they'll likely pull their trick right on the outside o' the one big loop we're usin'.'

'You run the show,' Malone directed. 'Get 'em surrounded. We want 'em alive and without any shooting.'

They rode down the line for only a short distance, and then Terpin ordered a halt. Dismounting and leaving their horses in a thick stand of pine, they moved forward on foot, Terpin describing the area where he expected the surveyors to be. In a matter of minutes they could see the pair working, their routine just the same as that Malone had observed earlier.

'Runnin' a damned careful line,' Terpin muttered. 'Figgerin' so close that they coulda fooled anybody. Let's go, boys. I'll take 'em from this side, bein' as how I ain't skinny enough to git through the brush like some o' the rest of yuh.' He snapped orders in what was a whisper for him but which left Malone wondering why the two surveyors didn't hear him. The four of them began to circle, Jiggers and Lafe taking the low side while Malone climbed to a position where he could look down on the workers at their mischief.

Terpin had the time figured out pretty closely. He was the one who actually moved in, his gun ready as he shouted, 'Hands up high, you bastards! Don't make no moves!'

Owens had been close to his partner when the interruption came, and he promptly took advantage of the situation. Seeing only one fat man facing them, he stepped behind Wren and went for his gun. Malone blasted a slug into the ground at the man's toes and added his voice to Terpin's. 'Git 'em up, dam-mit! Stop tryin' to hide behind your partner.'

After that it was easy. Wren's bitter cursing at Owens was almost as flu-ent as Terpin's casual appraisal of the pair of them. They were disarmed and searched, Terpin gleefully exhibiting the roll of bills he took from each man. They were bank notes of the Mountain Bank of Denver.

'Seems like this here Burchell sends out money like it was cheap stuff,' he laughed as he stuck the money into a shirt pocket. 'Mebbe I oughta see if he don't want to give me a bit of it direct. Kinda tedious havin' to track down the middleman all the time.'

'Don't we git none o' that?' Jiggers asked.

'Nope. There's a couple o' hosses around here, some place that'll be your share. You and Lafe. When yuh git a chance yuh kin look up that rustler who's blacksmithin' fer O'Boyle. He kin fix up the brands fer yuh.'

'Nice honest lot,' Malone commented.
'Fight fire with fire,' Terpin said with mock solemnity. 'Now let's git this here mess organized. First thing' — he turned to stare at the prisoners — 'we seen your work back along the line there, gents. Yuh're real good at it Now yuh're goin' to git a chance to be real good at puttin' them stakes right back where they belong. Exact, I mean! Now that I know yuh kin do it real good, yuh better not make no mistakes. We're kinda annoyed at yuh, so don't make me lose my temper.'

He kept his happy smile as he swung to Lafe and Jiggers 'Me 'n Lefty got to shove on over to O'Boyle's camp. We'll take these broncs and set things up fer yuh to git 'em later. Make camp here. Looks like there's plenty grub. We'll be back in the mornin' with more supplies and a scatter gun. After that yuh'll have all the time yuh need to watch a couple o' smart survey men puttin' stakes back where they belong. Think yuh kin handle it?'

Grins and nods from both Lafe and Jiggers gave him an answer, but he went on talking, clearly for the benefit of the prisoners. 'I'll be back again in a couple o' days, which oughta be time enough fur the job if'n yuh don't cripple 'em up none. If the job ain't done right when I check it out, then I'll do the cripplin'. Take turns watchin' while the other feller sleeps. At night tie up both o' the bastards. It ain't no skin off our butts if they git a mite cramped. It'll learn 'em not go git tangled up in this kind of a chore.'

Wren started to protest, but it only gave Terpin a chance to repeat his threats. 'Behave yuhrself and do the job,' he warned. 'That way yuh git outa this with a whole skin — more or less. Try any sneaky tricks, and I'll beat the livin' hell outa yuh personal!'

Malone asked quietly as Terpin led the way to the horses, 'What about our men being surprised by Hatfield? He could come out this way.'

'He ain't comin'. Not tonight. We'd know about it from Flannery by this time. Tomorrow we'll be movin' back where we can take care o' the bastard if he happens to be showin' up in this part of the country. I hope to hell it happens that way!'

Dusk was falling rapidly as they headed down the grade toward the upper camp. It wasn't long before they began to see where the survey had been brushed out in readiness for the graders. O'Boyle was moving rapidly. It would have been only a few days before he would have been led astray by the false markings. And Terpin felt sure that he would have been fooled. The trap was being well set at this point, perhaps even more cleverly than in the other two places.

He was talking with mixed admiration and anger about the way the job had been done when they rounded a little bend in the line and began to see workmen along an already graded line across a little valley. O'Boyle had his crew working late. Even though it was getting close to nightfall, they were just pulling back from where they had been grading out a line along this inside curve that connected two separate mountains.

'Happy bastards,' Terpin yelled at Malone, who was riding a little ahead. 'Look at 'em wavin' to us!'

Suddenly Malone knew that the waving on the far side of the hollow was not a cheerful greeting. He half-turned in his saddle to say what he thought, and at that moment the mountainside just ahead exploded. Malone was conscious of the concussion and then the noise. The rest of it never came clear in his mind. He knew that he had been hit in the face by a rock fragment, and he felt something burning at his left hand. None of it was too clear because he was having trouble keeping his mind clear to fight the frightened horse.

He didn't manage the complicated problem. He knew when he fell out of the saddle, but he didn't know when he hit the ground.

A pall of dust hung over everything when he got his wits about him again. It wasn't until he realized that Terpin was out of the saddle and bending over him that he knew he'd been unconscious. He tried to sit up and became aware of several other things, all of them painful His left arm hurt. So did his head. There was blood on the end of his nose.

'Lie down, yuh damned fool!' Terpin bellowed. 'Yuh're hurt.'

Malone remained sitting. It had taken pain to get there and he didn't want to have it all to do again. He tried to move the aching left arm and found that he couldn't do much with it. Then he noticed that the middle finger of his left hand was bent out of shape and that the hand was bloody. He didn't feel any pain there; probably it was numb.

He looked up at Terpin. 'How come you didn't get any of it?' he asked. 'You're a better target than me.'

The fat man grinned. 'I'm smart. I had yuh right in front of me.' He sobered to explain, 'Looks like O'Boyle was settin' off a blast so's his gang could clean up the mess first thing tomorrow. We ride right into it like a couple of greenhorns and we git yuh busted up.'

'How bad?'

'I ain't sure. Here comes Shawn and some of his boys. We'll git yuh back to camp and patch yuh up so's yuh'll hold water again. Take it easy.'

Malone was willing to let them handle him as they wanted to. He didn't have any strength in his legs, and it was a little hard to make his mind focus on anything. When he put his right hand to his forehead and felt the combination of lump and gash there, he could understand the feeling. Probably a bit of rock had caught him just above the right eye.

They lifted him into his saddle, the spooked horse having been caught easily enough by one of Shawn O'Boyle's workmen. Terpin rode close beside him, ready to help, but Malone made it to camp without collapsing. A couple of times he wanted to give up and fall off, but each time he swore at himself and hung on. Somehow the thing that bothered him most was that he had gotten himself hurt just when he needed to do a lot of things. That business about the bluff with Guinn. It ought to be followed up. And he didn't even know how he had planned to do it.

Then he was being eased from the saddle and half-carried into a tent at the grade camp. O'Boyle took over then, assisted by a skinny little man with a fringe of gingery whiskers around the point of his jaw, O'Boyle seemed to depend on the little man's judgment, so Malone foggily decided that he had to do the same.

'Not real bad,' the little man said in a reedy voice. 'Concussion, no doubt. Piece of rock just missed his eye. Hit him pretty hard. Worst part's the left elbow. Bad sprain. Seems funny. Bein' in the edge of a blast, you'd expect bruises and cuts, not sprains.'

'I fell off my horse,' Malone explained, trying not to sound comical and not doing a very good job of it.

'Bronc spooked when the blast went off,' Terpin cut in. 'Kinda stung by some flyin' rocks, I reckon. Like me. Malone was the only unlucky jigger to git hit by a big one.'

It all seemed logical enough, Malone decided in a hazy kind of way. A rock hits him over the eye. A horse bucks him off, and he falls with his left arm doubled under him. Somehow he was thinking about it as though it had happened to somebody else. He heard the little man comment about the finger having been broken and cut by flying stone — and it still seemed as though the talk was of someone else. Only the hurt was personal.

O'Boyle gave him a big slug of whisky before they started cleaning up the forehead wound. He got another when they started to set the broken finger. He wasn't sure about it, but he thought he drank at least another tumbler of the stuff while they were working on the twisted elbow. Somehow the elbow didn't hurt so much after that.

He opened his eyes to daylight showing through canvas. His head hurt. When he tried to move, he hurt in a lot of other places. His left arm had been strapped to his body, but it still hurt. So he lay still while he tried to piece things together in a mind that didn't seem to be very active. He wondered whether the fuzziness was the result of the bump or the whisky. He decided that it was probably due to both.

Some time later he found the little man with the ginger fringe standing over him, so he asked, 'Where's everybody?' It wasn't much of a question, but it was the one that came out.

'Don't worry about them. How do you feel?'

'Like something the cat dragged in and left under the stove.'

The little man laughed. 'You're all right. Can't be too groggy if you can dig up old jokes.'

'I'm groggy, all right. Hangover?'

'Likely. They poured a lot of liquor into you. A man needs liquor when he has a muleskinner for a doctor. Think you could do with a bit of broth? Cook's been keepin' somethin' hot. He calls it broth, but I ain't so sure but what it's dishwater.'

'I'll try anything. I've got to get up and going.'

'Don't fret yourself. You won't be goin' anywhere for a week.'

He went out before Malone could declare himself. Somehow it took a lot of effort just to talk.

Most of the day went by in that same uncomfortable haze. He knew that he swallowed some kind of soup that didn't taste too bad in spite of the jokes the bearded man had made about it. He knew that O'Boyle came along once and made more jokes, mostly about the out-law horse-doctor who was treating him. Malone had a vague feeling that there might be a bit of truth behind the jok-ing but he sensed that mostly they were trying to keep things cheerful. That part he didn't like. It was too much along the line of giving the condemned man a hearty meal. They must think he needed a lot of cheering.

It wasn't until the next day that his head cleared up. He still had fever, the bearded man told him, and they refused to let him get up. He didn't mind after one feeble attempt that made his head ache. When he asked about Terpin, he was told the fat man had left early the previous morning, keeping his promise to check on the way his guards were putting the prisoners to work.

'Don't keep proddin' yerself,' O'Boyle told him. 'Matt'll take care o' ever'thing. He said so hisself.'

'I can imagine! Have you had any word from Flannery about Hatfield?'

'Sure. Yestiday. Feller met Terpin along the trail, so we got a word on both of 'em. Matt's headin' back to the main camp. Hatfield took the train down to the junction the same day ye got yerself in the way o' thim rocks.'

After hearing that, Malone found it easier to relax. At least there was no immediate risk that the men guarding the captured surveyors wonld be surprised by Jim Hatfield. Evidently the gunman was on his way to report.

In a way, that only made his helplessness more irritating. Malone had baited

251

a trap and Hatfield was biting. Now the trap wasn't going to be sprung. It would be only a matter of days before the enemy would try something new — and this time it would probably be rough. Time was becoming a big factor for both sides. The accidents down the line had used up just about all the safety margin for the construction gangs.

Toward night he knew that he was feverish again. He couldn't make up his mind whether to feel triumphant at the thought that so far enemy activity had not cost the railroad much. He had done his job well in that respect partly because of luck and partly because of careful attention, but the general position was not good. This was the critical time, and he wasn't doing a thing to earn Hannibal Putnam's gratitude. Somehow that was what he wanted. He owed it to the old man.

Another day produced a lot of improvement. But the news was bad. There was a message from Hannibal Putnam. Old Put had gone out to Denver on a sudden hunch that he might scare up some new financing and also to make arrangements for proper repair of the locomotive. When he started trying to find extra money he had run into the story that the S. & F. had already gotten more financing. He had traced the report back to Burchell and Hatfield.

Malone could imagine what that little development would mean. He had not told Old Put about the bluff he'd run on Hatfield, and the old man had unknowingly spilled the beans. Now Burchell would know that he still had a chance to steal the line as he had planned. The fact that he had been jockeyed into buying a freight outfit he didn't want wouldn't make any difference in the long run. He still had those S. & F. bonds.

The next report came on the following day. Again it was from Putnam. He did not indicate that he had any knowledge about the matter of the two surveyors, but he seemed to understand why Malone was still at O'Boyle's camp and was letting him know every possible detail. His note read:

Brian Guinn has sold out for cash, I hear. Hatfield is operating the freight line and his first move was to stop all shipments of supplies to our people at Silverdale. No more ore coming out unless we pay double price. Hatfield brought three men with him when he came back from Denver. Hard cases.

Better let me know what you and Matt are trying to do. He didn't tell me a thing before he left. Flannery wants to know whether he should relieve the two men you left on duty in the mountains. Terpin sent extra supplies to them but we don't know what orders he gave.

It was signed 'Hannibal,' and the general tenor of it left Malone with a picture of a puzzled little man. He was almost as puzzled himself. Where had Terpin gone? And why?

That night he discussed it with O'Boyle, but the only additional information he could get was about the captured surveyors. O'Boyle had ridden out to take a look just as the two men were completing the restaking job. He gave a wryly humorous account of how the two guards had been amusing themselves with willow switches, flicking the calves of their victims to keep them on the jump. All he knew was that the proper survey stakes were once again in place and that the proper grade had been carefully set up. There had been no mention of what was to be done with the prisoners when their job was completed.

'I don't like it,' Malone told him. 'Terpin must know that the pair could make trouble for us over our seizure of their horses and money. He won't want to turn 'em loose alive.'

'Murder ain't Matt's line,' O'Boyle assured him. 'He's done some killin' in his day, I don't doubt, but it wasn't real murder. I'm thinkin' he's takin' 'em somewhere that won't be real happy fer 'em and where they won't be causin' no talk fer some time to come. That's mebbe why he didn't say nothin' to nobody when he left the main camp. Looks like even Flannery don't know what the big walrus is up to.'

'But you think he came up and joined Lafe and Jiggers to take the prisoners away?'

'Seems like. They ain't along the line nowhere. And Matt would make sure that they done their job right.' Malone had to take the opinion for what it was worth. Anyway, he couldn't afford to be worrying over a minor point. There were too many big ones that kept popping into his thoughts.

Another day brought even less optimism. No one had heard from Terpin, but there was a report that Jiggers and Lafe had been seen at Silverdale. The pair had bought some supplies at the mining camp, dodging questions but free with their money. They had bought quite a lot of food for only two men.

The obvious guess was that the surveyors were being held captive somewhere in the mountains, but nobody could come up with a decent explanation of why Terpin had ordered it that way or why he was going along with the two guards.

Wagons coming up the old trail with such loads as Hatfield permitted brought other reports, mostly contradictory ones. Hatfield had told his men that their jobs would be safe, but then he had fired about a dozen of the hands who had been hired away from the S. & F. He refused to handle railroad materials for the upper camp, but he was taking supplies to the miners at Silverdale. For some reason he chose to ignore the fact that the same company owned both the mines and the rail line.

Actually, little was being shipped, the wagon rates having been jacked so high that only the absolute necessities were being handled. To add to his pressure on the railroad people, Hatfield was demanding cash for every shipment. Maybe that was just another part of the squeeze, but Malone tried to take a bit of satisfaction from it. Possibly cash had become a problem with the new freight-line owners. Maybe one of the schemes that had come to his mind while he was helpless had a chance of working. The only way to find out was to get back out of the mountains and try.

He shook off the warnings of O'Boyle and the man with the ginger fringe. In nearly a week he had not heard the little man called by name. O'Boyle had begun to address him as Doc, and that was the end of it. Malone guessed that here was another man who wanted to keep his identity or his past a private matter, so he didn't press any questions. On this point his own sympathy was pretty close to the surface. All he wanted from the little man was an admission that for him to ride back down the gulch to Mule-skinn wouldn't stir up any more fever.

Doc finally agreed that it would be safe, so Malone left the tent for the first time in more days than he liked to count, He didn't know what was really happening at the Muleskinner camp. Terpin was still missing. Hatfield was obviously running the wagon outfit so as to hurt as much as possible any railroad operations in the mountains. The surveyors and their guards were still missing. The only good news was that Putnam had managed to get a quick repair job done on the leaky locomotive and that the engine was in service once more on a regular basis.

His last bit of preparation before leaving O'Boyle's camp was to re-rig his gun belt. It required a bit of work, fitting a holster to the right side and disposing of the one on the left, but O'Boyle's crew turned up a competent leather worker who did the job quite well. Malone didn't venture to try any fast draws from the right side while other men were looking at him. He knew that they would expect him to be awkward, merely using the right-hand gun as something to bring out in a real emergency. He hoped that he would not have to use it as well as he knew he could. Others besides Matt Terpin might begin to get ideas if they discovered that Lefty Malone was also pretty adept with his right hand. The thought still bothered him when he rode out of the camp, feeling a little unsteady in the saddle but anxious to get down to Muleskinner and find out what the contradictory reports meant. Somehow it seemed to him that events were shaping up for direct violence. Hatfield's importation of tough hands hinted in that direction. It was no time to have scruples about being ready to use a gun.

It helped his mood a little to see that

O'Boyle's gang had graded past the spot where he had been caught by the unexpected blast. Actually, they were past the stretch where the surveyors had been changing stakes at the time of their capture. It was a safe bet now that O'Boyle would grade through the pass well ahead of Flannery. The troubles south of the pass had set Flannery back a good two weeks, maybe three. It was a lucky thing that Terpin had persuaded Old Put to operate from both ends with the grading job. Otherwise those delays along the gulch would have ruined everything. Now there was still a chance — at least as far as he knew, Malone had to remind himself. Things might be in a worse mess than he suspected. With Terpin still missing, anything could have happened.

He found that riding wasn't as easy as he had expected it to be. That bit of fever had taken something out of him. He managed to slide from his saddle after getting through the pass, and rested at full length for some twenty minutes before he went on. It pleased him that he could mount his horse without too much trouble even though his left arm was still in a tight bandage and the splint on his finger made every movement awkward.

He followed the survey line so that he could take a look at the other two spots where the surveyors had worked so hard — twice. There was nothing that he could find that would give him any hint as to what had happened after the stakes were replaced properly. And they were back where they had beeen. So far as he could tell, they were right once more.

He found Flannery's advance men coming up the cliff top, cutting back into the slope a little deeper than had been planned. It was adding to the work schedule, but after that first rock fall it had seemed to be the only way to do it. He stopped to talk with the gang boss but learned nothing. There had been no new word from anywhere. Nobody knew what had happened to Matt Terpin. All the men knew was that Flannery was driving them hard, trying to make up some of the lost time.

Malone nodded and rode on. According to the mental schedule he had worked out, the graders ought to be well into the first big loop by this time. Instead, they were just beginning to work along the top of the long cliff. The rock slide and the engine breakdown had held them up that much. Now he decided that it might be wise to give O'Boyle a few more men and let him try to make his gang meet with the main crew somewhere out on the big loop. He'd mention the idea; they could turn it down if it didn't sound good to the men who knew what they were doing.

He found Flannery just below the bend where a new line had been graded out beyond the spot where the rock slip had occurred. Only a few yards farther along, men were unloading ties and rails from flatcars that had been pushed up the grade by the panting locomotive. At least the engine was back in service. It saved a lot of time to have material brought along in carloads instead of in wagonloads. Things seemed to have gotten back to something like normal. Late but normal.

Flannery even tried to sound humorous as he greeted, 'Howdy. I hear ye thought yer head was harder'n some o' Shawn O'Boyle's rocks.'

Malone put his hand gently to the patch on his forehead. 'It wasn't,' he admitted with a wry smile. 'Neither was my arm or my finger. Gettin' soft, I guess.'

Flannery gestured toward the bend in the grade. 'I reckon ye see how we had to do it. Took time, but I figger we're in the clear now.'

'How much time did it cost you?'

The lean features twisted into a frown. 'Near three weeks. Gonna be awful hard to make up.'

'What about the rest of the mess? I heard that Hatfield was getting tough about the wagons that have been supplyin' our other camp and the mines. Anything new on that?'

'Not that I heard of. We ain't sending much stuff up, but we'll have to figger out some way o' gittin' around it.'

'What happened to Matt? All I heard was that he'd disappeared.'

Flannery shook his head. 'I dunno a damned thing about it. All I know is that he got aboard the train without sayin' nothin' to nobody and went down to the Junction. Then on to Denver, I reckon.'

'When was this?' Malone asked in surprise. 'I didn't hear anything about him going by train. I guessed that he'd slipped away to help Lafe and Jiggers do something about those two pet survey-ors they were keeping on a leash.'

'Hell no! Lafe and Jiggers were back layin' track this mornin'. They're unloadin' stuff right now.' He motioned toward the crew that was removing rails from a flatcar. 'Matt left 'em their orders and let 'em work things out their own way.'

Malone didn't even look around. He was trying to guess what this bit of news meant. 'When did Matt leave?' he asked.

'Lemme see. I kinda git mixed up in the days with so much of a rush on all the time. Musta been the day after he rode back here and told us about ye gittin' caught in the explosion. Come to think of it, it had to be that day. That was when the engine went on down fer her repair job. We didn't git her back 'til yestiday.'

'And you don't know why he left?'

'Nope. He didn't even tell nobody he was goin'.'

Malone pulled a crooked grin. 'You making any guesses?' Flannery matched the grin. 'Nope. Most times I got some right good ideas about what that fat rascal is up to, but he left me flat on this deal.'

'You think Lafe or Jiggers might know? I probably ought to find out what they did with their tame surveyors.'

'No secret there. They claim Matt told 'em what to do and said he wouldn't be back to check up like he'd planned to do at first. So they let their prisoners talk 'em into turnin' 'em loose. The poor devils was scared Terpin would kill 'em even if they done their job real good — which it 'pears they did. Anyhow the boys herded 'em east fer about miles and turned 'em loose. Promised 'em that if they showed up around here or told anybody how they got away Terpin wouldn't ever git no chance to kill 'em 'cause Lafe and Jiggers would git the job done first.'

'Ten miles east? That's real wilderness. No trails within miles.'

Flannery chuckled. 'That's how the boys figgered it. Seems like a couple o' good surveyors with their instruments and a little grub oughta git out of place like that before they could starve.'

Malone rode on. He gave the former guards a wave and a grin as he passed, but he did not stop to talk. Generally it was better not to know too much about any arrangements that Terpin had made. Not in matters like this one.

He found both Putnam and his daughter at the S. & F. office, their preoccupation with routine work making everything seem so calm that he wondered why he had been doing so much worrying. Old Put probably had everything under control. He was a pretty shrewd fellow even if he had gotten in over his head in this attempt to branch out into big business.

There was a flurry of comment and explanation, mostly over the bandages that he wore, but finally he got down to the question he wanted to ask. 'Where did Terpin go? Why?'

Putnam stared. 'I thought maybe you knew. Seemed like it mighta been somethin' the pair of you cooked up while you were up there playin' sick at O'Boyle's camp.' The grin suggested that he wasn't intending any complaint.

'I don't know a thing about it. Don't you get any word from Denver nowadays?'

'Not lately. Train didn't run while the engine was in the shop. When she come back yesterday she was runnin' light and right from the repair shops. Today we needed her to get caught up on shovin' supplies up to the work gangs, so she didn't make a trip down to the Junction. I reckon nobody in Muleskinner has had any word from the outside for nigh onto a week. Why? You think Matt mighta got hisself into somethin' in Denver?'

'I don't know what to think. Right now I'm not quite sure of anything. Let's start by getting me straightened out on what has already happened and when.'

To his surprise it was Isabel who suggested, 'Why don't you come to supper with us? We'll be closing up here in about twenty minutes. I can put events in order for you and then maybe we can do some guessing as to what has been happening.' Her voice changed just a shade as she added, 'I think I can guess a part of it right now.'

'Thanks,' Malone told her. 'I'll go wash up.' He wasn't ready to talk about what he thought her guess concerned, but he had an uneasy feeling that it dealt with the story he had told Guinn and Hatfield. He hoped he could make his motives sound half as smart as they had seemed to him when he had tried the stunt.

Because he had it in mind, he started the supper talk by explaining all of his moves from the time he had first caught the surveyors changing the grade stakes. Putnam interrupted right in the beginning, but Malone waved him aside. 'I know I should have told you about it when I came here to get Matt, but it seemed to me that this was the kind of thing you'd be better off not to know about. Then you could always plead ignorance if we got into any legal tangle. Anyway, that's the way it was. Let me get on with the yarn.'

Isabel surprised him by being the one to comment when he finished. And that was two surprises in one evening. 'I told you that I'd guessed a part of this — and I was right. After what my father told me about the queer reaction he got to his attempts to find extra financing in Denver, I came to the conclusion that you had been telling some lies. It's too bad you didn't let him know about it; the trick might have worked.'

Malone nodded, grateful that he wasn't being judged too harshly. 'Trouble was I got myself bunged up and couldn't follow up the idea.'

'So I'll make a second guess, having been right on the first one,' the girl said, showing the smile that he had seeen only once before. She was enjoying the excitement now, although he didn't understand why. 'I think Mr. Terpin decided to do what you couldn't do. I think he went to Denver to put some pressure on the bank.'

'Why?' Malone asked. 'As I understand it, Terpin left here before Hatfield came back with the cash to buy out Guinn. Matt didn't know that our trick had put any strain on the bank's cash.'

'Maybe he expected that it would. Matt's pretty shrewd about things like that.'

Putnam was nodding his agreement. 'I think you're right, Iz. Matt expected the trick to work, and he wanted to be in Denver when the time was right. I wonder what he'll do?'

Malone grimaced. 'I was wondering what I was going to do — until it worked out that I couldn't do anything. Somehow all the ideas that came to me were

271

so crooked that I put them aside. Terpin wouldn't have such scruples.'

Isabel aimed that smile at him again. 'Mind telling me what you didn't want to do? I'm curious about consciences and how they work.'

'Well, I figured that the whole idea was that a bank short of cash would be in a jam if they were to have a run by depositors. I thought of several ways of starting that run, figuring that they would have to close their doors and have banking officials take over. We'd either run them out of business or tie them up so they couldn't cause trouble for a while.'

'And how did you plan to cause this run on the bank?' she persisted.

He grinned in some embarrassment. 'Starting rumors, for one thing. They tried it with their Indian scare talk; seemed like the idea might work both ways. I didn't think that would be enough, but I had a feeling that if I could follow that up by setting off some kind of a blast along the bank wall one night and getting word out that the place had been robbed it would . . . '

Putnam laughed loudly. 'Lefty, you're as crooked as Terpin! I'm plumb surprised at you.'

'Nothing of the sort,' Isabel scoffed. 'You're just sorry you didn't think of it. And that's where my other guess comes in. I'm guessing that Matt did. Maybe not that same idea, but one something like it.'

The elder Miss Putnam got into the conversation for the first time since she had given Malone a formal but reasonably friendly greeting. 'I think,' she said acidly, 'that I have gotten myself mixed up with a band of absolute criminals. And that includes my niece, who seems to condone such unlawful deeds,' Then she smiled and added calmly, 'I trust that our Mr. Terpin will have handled the matter efficiently.'

15

It was late when Malone finally made his way to his cot in the warehouse. The talk had lasted several hours, everyone trying to get a clear picture of their situation. Some of it was easy. Construction had reached a stage where normal progress would see them through just about in time. They could not stand another serious accident or deliberate interference with the work schedule.

The rest was not so clear. They could only guess what might have happened in Denver. They had to make guesses on the subject of Hatfield's next moves. The fact that he had brought in some pretty ugly characters hinted that he might be planning to disrupt work schedules by some sort of threats to S. & F. workmen. As operator of the wagon company, Hatfield would have plenty of chance to try a lot of things.

'Nothin' to do but to keep pushin',.'

Putnam summed it up. 'While we push rail into the mountains, we just keep our eyes skinned, ready to fight off whatever gets aimed at us.'

'Seems like I made things worse than they were,' Malone grumbled. 'I prodded Hatfield into buyiug Guinn out. Now we've got Hatfield in a stronger position than before. I was the one who talked a lot of nonsense about busting the Mountain Bank. If Terpin gets us all tossed into the Federal pokey for what he's trying up there, that'll be my fault, too.'

'Sounds like your arm must be getting sore,' Isabel Putnam said with a wry smile. 'Better get some rest. You won't feel so sorry for yourself in the morning.'

They had ended it on that almost humorous note, but Malone didn't think that he was going to get much sleep. The more he thought about the whole deal the more he became convinced that he had made a mess of it.

Nonetheless, he fell asleep almost as soon as he eased himself between the blankets. Weakness and the physical strain of riding more than offset the worries that nagged at him. The elbow ached — just as Isabel Putnam had guessed — but it couldn't keep him awake. It seemed to him that he hadn't even gotten himself comfortable for the night when he heard Flannery's men singing as they climbed aboard flatcars to be transported up to the work area.

He listened sleepily, dreading to make the moves that would bring stiff and aching muscles into action, and caught some of the words the men were singing.

There's blaggards a-plenty up Mule-
    skinner way,
A-tryin' to wreck our railroad job.
But Lefty and Matt fight dirty their
    selves,
They're the boys who kin give 'em a
    belt in the gob.
We'll build the line no matter who
Keeps messin' around wid their dirty
    tricks.

We're Flannery's gang wid a whack-
    hurroo
We'll fight 'em wid shovels and mat-
    tocks and picks.
Wid me philalloo, hubbaboo, whack
    hurroo, boys . . . '

'Seems like I've been adopted,' Malone said to himself aloud. 'Maybe I'd better stir around a bit and start earning some of the confidence they seem to have in me.'

It wasn't so easy. Every move hurt at first, but by the time he had had some breakfast he was limbering up fairly well. Only the left arm and hand remained sore, but that he had to expect.

The little locomotive was backing down to the temporary yards when he left the cook shack, and he saw that the trainmen were getting ready to pick up a string of empties instead of shoving more loaded cars up to the work site. Evidently the trip to the junction was to be made during the morning instead of late in the afternoon, as had been the habit in recent weeks.

Putnam came out of the office, and Malone went on down the track to meet him. 'Sending the train down early?' he asked. 'Won't Flannery need the engine to keep his supplies coming up?'

Putnam shook his grizzled head. 'He's got everything he needs 'til about noon. We oughta be back by that time.'

'You mean you're going?'

'Sure. I got to know what the hell mess Terpin has stirred up in Denver. I'll use the D. & R. G. telegraph at the junction. Rather that than to stew around here wonderin'.'

Malone merely nodded. Putnam didn't have his worries without having company.

The train headed down toward Fremont Junction some ten minutes later, carrying no passengers except Hannibal Putnam. Malone stopped in at the office long enough to get a couple of bits of information from Isabel Putnam, mainly in an attempt to straighten his mind out on the sequence of events during his absence from Muleskinner. It

278

was a little difficult to see how so much had happened so quickly. Terpin had followed Hatfield in a hurry, but the lean gunman had been back with cash within forty-eight hours. And Guinn had made his sale in less time than that.

'Hatfield left here on a Thursday,' Isabel told him. 'Matt followed on Friday. Hatfield was back Saturday. Guinn left Monday. That should help you get the time in mind.'

'Not quite. Flannery said that Matt went down on the trip when the engine was going to the repair shop. How did Hatfield get back here next day?'

'On a horse, of course! He rode up from the junction with those plug-uglies as his guards. At first we thought he'd hired men to come with him because he was carrying money. Then we found out that he was keeping them on for some purpose we haven't found out about yet.'

'Then Guinn left on a horse? Carrying that money?'

'Exactly. He seemed to understand the man he was dealing with. At any rate he also traveled under guard, using men who didn't want to stay here and work for Hatfield. I hear that he made some pretty pointed remarks about how he proposed to defend himself if anybody tried to take the cash away from him.'

'And you think he got out with it?'

She shook her head. 'We've heard nothing to the contrary — but then we haven't heard much on any subject since that time. All I know is that Hatfield and his bruisers didn't leave Muleskinner. So I think Mr. Guinn probabably made it to the junction all right.' She let a thin smile come to her lips as she asked, 'Would I be asking too much to inquire about how you happen to be so well acquainted with men like this Hatfield?'

Malone chuckled. 'No harm in asking. But the answer don't mean much. Kinda like if I asked you how you happened to be on such good terms with a rascal like Matt Terpin. And Matt's a real rascal, you know. He brags about it.'

'So I get an evasive answer. Very well. I shouldn't have asked.'

Malone decided that the social call had run its course. 'No harm done,' he told her as he headed for the door. 'You didn't get any answers.'

He spent a couple of hours studying the material piled up along the sidings. He could only estimate the quantities still to be used and it was not his job anyway, but it served to keep him busy. Moving around was better than sitting down and letting those sore muscles stiffen up again.

Noon had not yet arrived when he heard the locomotive whistle. Evidently the train crew had drilled off their empties and picked up loaded cars in the time it had taken Putnam to get his telegrams through. Either that or Terpin had been at the junction ready to return. Malone hoped that it would turn out to be the latter possibility.

When the train came in, only one passenger dropped down from the single coach. Hannibal Putnam was wearing a grin, and Malone felt better. Whatever the little man had heard was good news.

Isabel came out of the office, meeting her father at the same time that Malone did. Neither of them had to ask a question. The little man practically shouted his story at them. The telegraph hadn't carried much detail, but something had happened to the Mountain Bank of Denver. There had been a heavy wave of withdrawals by depositors, and the bank had attempted to close its doors. A riot had followed, and the bank had been overrun by men who wanted money. Some of them were probably entitled to get it, but just as surely a lot of hoodlums had joined the mob to become part of a wholesale bank robbery. Not that many of them had gotten away with much. The cash had virtually been gone before the mob broke in.

'Law got control after a spell, I understand,' Putnam concluded. 'They closed the place and passed the word that they found a lot o' things that wasn't on the level. Like I said, no details yet.'

'Was I right?' Isabel exclaimed triumphantly. 'I told you Matt would do it!'

'Funny thing,' her father said. 'I didn't want to put too many personal questions on the wire, but I couldn't get any hint that anybody named Terpin was mixed up in the mess.'

Malone laughed. 'Naturally. Matt never gets caught in any of that kind of trickery. He's smart.'

'And efficient.' The girl was still crowing.

'Better not let yer aunt hear you talkin' like that,' Hannibal warned with a chuckle. 'She'll think the country's plumb ruined yer morals.'

It wasn't until they were inside the office that the little man exclaimed, 'One thing I didn't tell you. Mark Wheeler was down at the junction. Been waitin' there for two days for a train. I wouldn't let him aboard, and the last I knew he was tryin' to hire a horse. Seems like he was in all-fired pucker to get up here and tell Hatfield all about it.'

'More likely he was sent to see if he could get back some of the cash they paid Guinn,' Malone commented.

'Then he's too late. Guinn caught a train to Denver a couple o' days ago. Mebbe more'n that. I didn't ask too close. Anyway he's gone — and he took the money with him.'

Malone headed for the door. 'I think I'd better find Flannery,' he remarked cheerfully. 'He'll be interesed in the news, and I imagine he'll want to make sure that he's got a man or two hanging around the bar when Wheeler shows up there.'

They went through the afternoon in an atmosphere of repressed excitement. On the surface the news was good. The enemy was in trouble. But no one wanted to assume too much. Until more information could be obtained, they could not be certain that some last frantic move might not be made in an effort to retrieve the disaster that had overtaken the plotters.

There had been no change in the situation when Malone gave up and went to bed. He knew that he had to take account of his own weakness. Another day might bring more demands than he would physically be able to meet.

Flannery roused him a little after midnight. 'I figgered ye oughta know,' the grade boss told him. 'There's been somethin' doin' over at the Muleskinner. Wheeler got in about the time ye went to sleep. Seems like he got lost in the dark or somethin' and he was a mite scratched up.'

Malone was awake in an instant. 'Hear anything about Denver?'

'Nope. All my man could tell me was that Wheeler went into another room with Hatfield. They was alone mebbe twenty minutes to a half hour. Then Hatfield started gittin' his stuff together.'

'Packing up to leave?'

'That's it. And he's gone. Took them new fellers with him. Seemed like Wheeler wanted to go along, but they told him he was all tired out and couldn't keep up. When he started to argue, Hatfield knocked him flat and left him on the floor.'

'Didn't anybody get anything from

Wheeler after that?'

'Nope. He locked hisself up in the place where Guinn used to have his office set up. Won't talk to nobody.'

Malone was getting his feet into his boots. 'Maybe we can make him change his mind. I kinda think he oughta scare pretty easy. Want to give it a try?'

Flannery grinned happily. 'About time I got in on some of the fun. Matt raises hell in Denver. Lafe and Jiggers have theirselves a picnic in the mountains. I don't do nothin' but holler at gradin' gangs.'

'Get ready to holler some more,' Malone chuckled. 'If Wheeler's the lad I think he is — and he's as tired out as your man reports — it won't take much more than a good holler.'

He was right. The Muleskinner Hotel was closed when they reached it, worried employees having wisely decided to stay clear of any more trouble that the night might bring. Malone remembered the location of Guinn's office so he simply worked his way around to that side, counting windows. Then he rapped on a dark pane and warned, 'Might as well let us in, Wheeler. It'll make a lot less noise than if we have to break this window. Maybe we won't be quite so rough on you if you play along.'

There were a few moments of silence before a fearful voice whispered, 'Who's out there?'

'Malone. And Flannery. You know we don't fool around.'

'Hold it. I'll let you in the front door.'

Flannery chuckled in the darkness. 'Scared outa his wits. Seems like he oughta talk without no trouble at all.' It was easier than either of them had expected. Wheeler led them to the office, where he had already lighted a bracket lamp. They could see that he had been going through an untidy lot of papers that Hatfield probably had left behind him. Mr. Wheeler was not the slick individual ho had been when he had been the S. & F. supply chief. Now his hair was standing in every direction. There was a purple bruise beginning to puff under one eye. His clothing was torn, stained, and rumpled. Malone remembered that the man had slept one night in the open shelter at Fremont Junction before making the ride up the wagon trail.

'What do you want of me?' Wheeler asked in a helpless voice.

'The truth. All of it. We want to know what happened in Denver. We want to know what message you brought to Hatfield. We want to know what he's planning to do now. I'll warn you that we know enough to catch you in any lie you might try. So start talking!'

'No point in lying,' the man said bitterly. 'I suppose you heard how I got this.' He poked tentatively at the bruise. 'I tried to help the man who'd been paying me. This is the thanks I got.'

'Don't expect any sympathy from us,' Malone warned him. 'Get the yarn told.'

Wheeler let them have it quickly. He had been working at the Mountain Bank after leaving Muleskinner. He knew that Hatfield had come down to Denver and had gone into a rather lengthy conference with Burchell. Then Hatfield had gone away with so much cash that the bank had begun trying to call in some loans so their cash supply wouldn't be so dangerously short. Wheeler had personally visited two other bankers in the city in an attempt to get additional cash.

That was when they first began to hear of the rumors that were going around. People with bank notes of the Mountain Bank were practically apologizing when they offered the notes in trade, giving the impression that they expected tradespeople to refuse them. In no time at all that was the way it worked out. Word spread that such notes could not be redeemed. Storekeepers wouldn't take them. People began to bring them to the bank for redemption throwing additional strain on the depleted cash reverses.

By the second day, and before anybody could find out what had started the talk, the rumor had gained in size. Now it was being whispered that the Mountain Bank had issued great quantities of worthless paper money. Another report was that the bank had invested heavily in a freighting company that was on the verge of going out of business.

The Mountain Bank did not survive that second day. Depositors began to make wholesale withdrawals, refusing to take the bank's currency. By noon the cash supply was gone. Other banks refused help, and the word went out that the Mountain Bank had been turned down in its efforts to borrow. There was nothing to do but to close the doors.

At that point there was a line of people waiting to take out money, a long line that extended halfway down the block. When the doors closed the line became a mob. Before the law could take a hand, the mob rushed the bank, broke open the doors, and began to make withdrawals in its own way. Unquestionably, plenty of hoodlums had joined the mob in an effort to get in on a safe kind of bank robbery, but they hadn't gotten much. By that time there had been nothing for them to get.

'No money, at least,' Wheeler said in

a grim tone. 'But somebody got into Burchell's desk and got away with some papers that really set up a lot of trouble. Maybe you know about how Burchell and Hatfield got into the bank business?'

'By fraud and murder,' Malone said promptly.

Wheeler looked surprised. 'I didn't know it until the papers turned up in the office of the Federal District Attorney. I never did hear how they got there.'

Malone didn't comment. He thought he could have explained, just as he could have explained about the quantity of Mountain Bank money that had been spent in starting the rumors. Matt Terpin had been a busy fellow.

'So Burchell was grabbed by Federal marshals,' Wheeler concluded. 'He passed me the word to warn Hatfield. I was to tell Jim so he could avoid arrest. If it wasn't too late, I was to tell him to back out of the Guinn deal and salt the money away for legal defense. I guess you know I was too late.'

'And Hatfield ran out on you?'

'Right. He took his thugs and rode down the wagon trail an hour ago.'

No one said a word. Then Flannery drawled, 'Now ain't that a damned shame!'

16

They left Wheeler to his miseries. There
didn't seem to be any point in getting
Putnam out of bed to tell him what had
happened, so they simply went back to
their own cots and turned in for the rest
of the night. Malone was only too happy
to settle himself again. He ached in so
many places that it was hard for him to
realize that the battle was won. He still
wasn't quite sure how it had been won,
but the enemy was on the run. Nothing
else counted. He couldn't even feel dis-
gruntled that Terpin had taken the play
away from him. The big thing was that the
railroad line was out of danger and there
had been no demand on Lefty Malone
to do anything that might remind anyone — except Terpin — of Jack Kyle.

He slept soundly after the excitement
died out of him, awakening in the gray
dawn with the feeling that he was dream-
ing. He had imagined that he'd heard a

locomotive whistle in the distance. With the S. & F. engine hissing gently not a hundred yards from the warehouse, it was obviously something out of a dream.

Now he heard it again, and this time he was sure of it. He could not guess what it meant. He slipped out of his blankets and crossed to a window to make sure that the S. & F. engine was actually on its siding, its fires banked. After that he went to the door and stood in the morning chill long enough to know that this was no dream. He could hear a locomotive laboring on the long grade.

Several other men appeared in various stages of undress, and questions began to fly back and forth. Malone didn't wait to get into the useless conversation. He hobbled back to the cot and began to work his way into his clothes. There could be only one explanation: This was a D. & R. G. engine coming up the grade. It was a risky proposition for the larger road to send a train onto a spur where the S. & F. was accustomed to running its own equipment without fear of collision.

The way the Rio Grande engineer was keeping his whistle going suggested that he knew the danger involved. Obviously this was some kind of emergency, or the D.R.G. wouldn't have made the move.

By the time Malone made his way down the track toward the office, the approaching engine was coming around the last bend below the gulch, her whistle still shrieking its nervous warnings. Flannery swung in beside Malone, his lean features hiding a tinge of curiosity behind dry humor. 'Sounds almost as loud as Matt Terpin,' he commented. 'I wonder if the fat rascal has stole himself a engine?'

'We'll soon find out,' Malone replied. 'She's in sight. Just an engine. No cars.'

'Hope we git it over fast. My whole damned gang's out gawkin'. Kitchen bitches, too. We won't git finished breakfast and out on the job 'til the mornin's half gone.'

'Cheer up. Maybe we can afford that much delay. Remember?'

Flannery nodded, his grin coming

295

back. 'Have ye told Old Put?'

'Haven't had time to tell anybody. Maybe I'd better fill him in fast before that engine gets here.'

He left Flannery abruptly and went across to where all three Putnams stood watching the approaching locomotive. It struck him as vaguely significant that only Miss Hannah Putnam had found time to put on regular clothing. Hannibal was notably comical in a red wool robe that was not long enongh to hide the night-shirt underneath. It wasn't the robe or the nightshirt that provided the comedy. That feature came from the combination of a pair of fancy bedroom slippers and the big Texas hat. Malone guessed that the slippers belonged to one of the women, but the big hat looked just as grotesque.

Isabel was just as hastily clad, but in her case the impression was pleasant rather than humorous. With the dark hair in a braid and a big fuzzy robe covering her from neck to heels, she looked like a particularly attractive Indian squaw. Not the kind Malone had seen in the Indian villages but the kind the artists put in the pictures they sold back East.

He caught her quick smile of greeting but hurried into the explanation he wanted to make. It occurred to him that she had been better than cordial lately, probably because she regretted the way she had talked to him on the subject of Mark Wheeler. He couldn't afford to let anything develop between them, so he made his report a little more brisk than necessary, trying to cover the impression with the idea that he had to get his story told before the Rio Grande engine could reach them. With everyone so curious about the unexpected arrival, it was not too difficult.

Even before he finished they were all watching the locomotive's cab as the engineer applied his brakes. They could see the fireman leaning out from the gangway on their side of the track, and they could tell that several other men were riding in the cab. It was only when the engine ground to a shuddering halt directly in front of them that they recognized the bulky form of Matt Terpin taking up the space of two or three men.

The fireman and a stringy man whose air of authority hinted that he was the conductor of this irregular run came down to the ground first. They gingerly assisted Terpin out of the cab and then stood back while two men with rifles dropped to the trackside gravel.

Terpin promptly took charge. He was sooty, unshaven, red-eyed. He seemed to be having trouble making tired legs support so much body, but he managed to be impressive. 'Mr. Putnam's right over there, gents,' he told the strangers in his best bellow. 'Take it up with him.'

He started the pair toward Putnam but didn't stop shouting. 'All of you train monkeys git on the job. I promised the Rio Grande folks that we'd git their engine back to 'em in a hurry. Hustle up wood and water. They need that damned teakettle to keep their business runnin'.'

By that time he was within ten feet of Putnam and the others. 'Boss, these two gents are Federal marshals. Grayne and

Mulloy. I'll let 'em tell yuh why they're here.'

The taller of the two men nodded but made no attempt to follow up the informal introductions. 'We want a man named Hatfield,' he said abruptly. 'Your man Terpin pulled some strings and got the Rio Grande to send an engine up here so we could save time. Now we're hoping you can put us on Hatfield's track.'

Putnam motioned toward Malone. 'Better talk to Art Malone, gents. He just got done tellin' me about Hatfield.'

Malone repeated his story briefly, omitting any parts that had to do with his personal interests. All these men wanted was to get on the track of a fugitive murderer. That was the charge, they explained. In the wreck of the Mountain Bank there had been evidence that Hatfield had committed a murder in getting control of a mining operation some years earlier. They had a warrant for his arrest.

The Federal men didn't waste time in idle talk. They asked for information about the trails and then headed across toward the Muleskinner Hotel, pausing only to thank Terpin once more for using his influence to get them the Rio Grande engine for the trip up to Muleskinner.

When they were out of earshot, Malone stared at the fat man, a smile twisting the corners of his mouth. 'Seems like we got plenty of questions to ask you, Matt, but for a starter, how about explaining how it happened that you've got so much influence with the D.R.G. that they let you have an engine. I noticed that it wasn't the Federal Government who got the engine; it was Matt Terpin.'

Terpin winked broadly. 'No point in knowin' railroad directors if'n yuh can't git some favors done. Gov'ment coulda got the engine, all right, but I figgered I could save 'em a bit o' time. Seems like I didn't save 'em enough.'

Isabel Putnam put in a comment, her smile as quizzical as the one Terpin was wearing. 'By any chance,' she inquired, 'was this director who provided the engine the same one who might have been planning to arrange for the Rio Grande to buy up our line from Burchell?'

Terpin's grin faded. 'Somebody's been gittin' things figgered out,' he complained. 'Mebbe I don't need to tell nobody nothin'.'

Malone suddenly became aware of the men who had moved in to listen. 'Not now, anyway,' he said. 'Get your men to work, Flannery. We've got a railroad to build. Let the lawmen take care of Hatfield.'

He could say it with real relief. Somehow he had had a feeling that Hatfield would be his personal problem, a problem that would require the Kyle manner of handling.

For the next hour affairs moved so swiftly that there was no time to press Terpin for any answers. Flannery rushed his men through a belated breakfast. The S. & F. train crew worked with the Rio Grande men in getting the engine ready for its return trip. There had been some question as to whether the locomotive was to wait and take the marshals back with their prisoner, but word quickly came that the lawmen were getting horses and would ride down the wagon trail after Hatfield. The Rio Grande engine had done its chore; as soon as it could be loaded with wood, its crew fed, it could go back to regular duty.

Terpin explained what the two marshals had in mind with their apparently useless pursuit of Hatfield. It had been anticipated that Wheeler might have brought the alarm to the wanted man and that Hatfield would have fled. In the event that he should try to get back to the rail line and head for distant country, the marshals were prepared. Two of them were to come up the trail and set up a trap, while the other pair rode the Rio Grande engine in hopes of getting their man before he could start.

'I jest hope they listened to what I tole 'em,' the fat man growled. 'Hatfield and them plug-uglies o' his'n ain't likely to give up easy. I warned the lawmen to throw down on 'em from cover if that was the way it happened to work out.' He beamed virtuously as he added, 'I don't like to see no lawmen git hurt doin' their duty.'

'Not in a deal where you supplied the Federals with their evidence,' Malone agreed quietly. 'You've been a busy man, Matt.'

'How do yuh know so goddam much?' Terpin demanded irritably. 'I figgered I didn't show in none o' this.'

'Physically you didn't — which is a pretty good trick for a man of your build — but the Terpin style sticks out in every dirty little detail.'

'Tryin' to sound smart, hey? Mebbe yuh think yuh know how it all worked out.'

'I don't think I'm far wrong on most of it — but wait until Isabel Putnam gets a chance to question you. She's been doing some pretty clever guessing, and I imagine she'll try to pin you down on a couple of points.'

Terpin stared. 'What's been happenin' around here? Hell! The last time you and her got near each other, there wasn't nothin' but spit flyin'. Now yuh make it sound like yuh think she's all right.'

'That's just about it. But no more than that. Don't start trying to imagine things.'

'Why the hell not? Everybody else is imaginin' all over the place.'

They had moved out of the warehouse as they talked, watching as the S. & F. engine started up the grade with its load of workmen and materials. The Rio Grande locomotive had pulled in on a siding while the work crew got into action, but now it began to steam slowly toward the switch, ready to back down to the junction.

Terpin let out a guffaw. 'Look who's figgerin' to ride down on the visitin' engine!' he exclaimed. 'Them fancy wimmen ain't gonna look so damned fancy when they git a lot o' ashes in their hair rats.'

Tillie Atherton and her colleagues seemed to have made a hasty decision. Tillie herself was running with her red hair streaming down her back. The broken-nosed blonde appeared to be wearing a nightgown under a long coat. All of them were carrying garments that they had not taken time to pack.

'Marshals must have scared 'em,' Malone said idly. 'Or maybe they just decided that the Muleskinner wasn't going to be having any big rush of paying customers in the future.' He hoped he wasn't sounding too smug about it. Somehow it pleased him as much to get Tillie and her memory out of the way as to see the end of Jim Hatfield. Maybe Jack Kyle could safely be counted as dead.

'Interestin' thing there,' Terpin remarked in a suspiciously soft tone. 'The towhead's wearin' a nightgown. I wouldn't ha' figgered she ever had use fer one.' He sighed ponderously and added, 'Must be they changed the rules o' the whores' union since I was a young feller.'

The Rio Grande crew didn't offer much objection to their new passengers. Even the engineer climbed down to help boost the anxious quartet into the cab. Since the boosting was done with vast enthusiasm, there was an abrupt change in the voices of the women. By the time the engine started to back down the grade toward Fremont Junction, it seemed like a fair guess that this was going to be quite a trip.

'Ten to one that damned engineer fakes a breakdown before he gits to the junction,' Terpin growled.

'Ten to one on a sure thing! No, thanks.'

By that time the valley was quiet. The marshals had disappeared down the wagon trail, evidently leaving Wheeler to fret alone at the hotel. The construction crew was out of sight, ready to do a normal day's work. Malone found himself at a loss; he didn't have a thing to worry about.

'Let's go see the Putnams,' he suggested. 'It's time we worked out the happy little details of how the Mountain Bank happened to go bust.'

Terpin grinned. 'I don't mind if I do. I'm gettin' curious as hell to find out what all this guessin' is about.'

They were greeted happily by both Putnams when they went into the office. Today seemed to be the day for everyone to be smiling. Certainly the luck had turned and there was plenty to smile about.

Hannibal Putnam elected to be heavily facetious. 'Well, if it ain't Mr. Terpin, the friend of railroad directors! Welcome, Mr. Terpin. Do you figure you could visit with a few common folks for a spell and explain a few little matters of high finance — like how to bust a bank?'

Terpin grinned. 'Seems like I ain't gonna git the chance. Lefty seems to have it all worked out that Miss Iz tells me all about it. Seems like her and him have got everything all figgered out.'

'Don't feel bad, Matt,' the girl laughed. 'It's just that we thought we could see your hand in those operations. And I finally made some good guesses and I'm a little proud of myself. After being wrong at first, it gives me a chance to look a little more intelligent.'

Terpin frowned. This wasn't the way he had expected the talk to go. 'What guesses, ma'am?' he asked.

'About our troubles. I felt sure that it was Guinn behind it all. I thought you and Malone were stupid to believe in somebody else behind him. And I was wrong about Mark Wheeler, so wrong that I said some things that weren't very diplomatic.'

'Not even polite,' Malone added, his smile taking any sting out of the words.

'Go ahead and crow,' she retorted. 'I checked the records as you suggested. That shipment that went astray was already recorded as having reached here. Because we found it in time, there was no damage done, but it gives you an idea of what he was trying to do. I also found some notes that make me think that he gave out information that would let those surveyors pick out the places where false grades could most easily be run. He also seems to have passed along information about the powder shipment.'

'What kind of notes?' Malone asked.

'Seems like something he wouldn't put in writing.'

'Just notes. Apparently to himself, perhaps as a reminder for making his claims for pay. I found them with waste that had been missed when the usual trash-burning took place.' Her smile was bright as she added, 'You see, I really took inventory. Even the trash piles.'

It gave Malone a feeling of embarrassment that she should be bidding so frankly for his good will. He couldn't afford to let anything develop between himself and a girl like Isabel Putnam. Not with his background. 'Tell Matt how you think he did it,' he said quietly. 'He's not much interested in Wheeler.'

She gave him a look that showed she was puzzled but then went on to make her guesses. Terpin had distributed the confiscated Mountain Bank currency among friends who had orders to use it immediately and to hint that they were expecting the merchants to refuse it. Then he had planted more friends in the line that formed as depositors became

309

fearful. Finally he had put a trusted lieutenant at the task of taking the private papers out of the bank's office. The papers that Burchell had been holding as a means of keeping Hatfield honest were sent to the Federal District Attorney. Other papers had been used to blackmail a Rio Grande director into providing a locomotive.

'I could make some more guesses,' she concluded, 'but I'm limiting myself to matters that concern our interests.'

Terpin's grin had broadened as she talked. Finally he turned to old Put and shook his head sadly. 'It's a awful thing, Mr. P., to find out yuh've brung up a gal what's got sech a head fer crime. Such a imagination!'

'Tell me just one thing I had wrong!' she challenged.

The fat man's grin faded. 'Most of it,' be said solemnly. 'Not that it didn't happen kinda like that. But I didn't do it.'

'Hah!' The exclamation was eloquent.

'All that happened was I paid up some debts I owed, bein' honest enough to tell the creditors that I wasn't none too sure about them notes. Now it jest so happens that my social circle ain't made up o' real sterlin' characters, and when them polecats went out to spend Mountain Bank notes like they was afraid they'd git arrested fer doin' it, they sure as hell got folks to thinkin'. Them apes couldn't spend gold money without havin' people think they was gittin' yeller lead!'

'And I suppose you didn't have *much* to do with the attack on the bank?'

'Practical nothin'. I jest happened to run across the feller what went through Burchell's safe. He showed me the stuff he hauled out of it. Even a crooked imagination like some folks around here have got wouldn't set yuh up to believe half o' the dirty deals on record there. Seems like this here Burchell was figgerin' two ways. If him and Hatfield could steal the S. & F., all to the good. If things went wrong, he had it fixed to let Hatfield take a fall while he took over the bank. That's why he was holdin' that evidence about the killin' Hatfield had done.'

'But why was the District Attorney so interested in Burchell if he had covered his tracks so well?' Malone asked.

'The bast — er — polecat was greedy. He'd played fast and loose with the bank-note game. I didn't lie to nobody when I said mebbe them notes wasn't much good. They wasn't.'

Putnam chuckled. 'You're soundin' damned near self-righteous, Matt. It don't become you.'

'I'm reformed,' Terpin told him solemnly. 'This here mess shows me that crime don't pay.'

'Hah!' It was Isabel again. She seemed to speak for all of them.

There was a moment of silence, all of them apparently content to let a sense of satisfaction have its way. Then Hannibal Putnam said quietly, 'I guess we're on the safe side now. Even if we hit the kind of trouble that we got to expect in this business, we won't be gettin' pressed by any bondholders. When the Government starts tryin' to clean up a busted bank, it takes 'em forever and a day.

Not likely we'll need to redeem bonds 'til we're runnin' the line and makin' a profit.'

'Funny thing,' Terpin said, his tone so elaborately innocent that Malone knew at once that something big was coming, 'that stupid . . . feller what busted into the safe told me that there was a whole bundle o' bonds in there. Forgeries, he claimed. They was all fancied up, he claimed, with big letters S. & F. on 'em. Everybody knows that there ain't no 'and' sign between the S. and the F. in Santa Fe, so he knowed they was fakes right away. Put a match to 'em so no more innercent victims would git swindled.'

There wasn't very much for anybody to say after that. Isabel didn't even have the energy for another 'Hah!'

By midday everything was back to something like normal. All of them were working at the business of getting the construction program set up for the big push across the pass, but they couldn't forget the way fortune had turned. Matt

Terpin had done a job. Not that he admitted it, but no one had much doubt as to how he had planned and executed it.

Putnam sent the engine down to the junction a little earlier than usual, partly because he wanted to get any new word that had come out from Denver and partly because they were growing concerned over the Hatfield matter. Four Federal officers against the five in Hatfield's party didn't shape up so good, even when the lawmen were warned and would have the advantage of surprise.

The word was not too good. There had been a brisk fight along the wagon trail only about a mile from Fremont Junction. At first the outlaws had pretended to surrender, but then, discovering that only two men were holding guns on them, they had put up a fight.

The two marshals who had set up the ambush were grim about it, obviously remembering Terpin's warning. At the first show of opposition, they had blasted away, killing two of the Hatfield gunmen and wounding a third. Hatfield and another man, believed to be a horse thief named Wicker had gotten away.

A second fight had occurred when the fugitives tried to double back toward Muleskinner. This time the lawmen had been out in the open, and Hatfield's gun skill had been too much for them. Grayne had been killed, and his partner had not been able to prevent the escape of the outlaws. The report was that Hatfield and Wicker had been riding hard toward the lower end of the S. & F. line when last seen. Fremont Junction was being guarded by armed men in the event that the pair should attempt to board a Rio Grande train there.

'Looks like we celebrated too soon,' Malone commented when he heard the report. 'They could head back here as well as toward Fremont.'

'Why?' Isabel asked. 'I should think they'd try to avoid a dead-end like this.'

'Maybe they've got a couple of reasons. They'll know that the main line will be watched. Up here we might not expect them. And maybe they know of a trail out of here. The surveyors seemed to have something like that in mind; they didn't seem to plan on coming back to Muleskinner. Also, a couple of men on the dodge will need supplies. This is the place they could get them.'

'I'm postin' men all around the place tonight,' Terpin told them. 'Might as well play it as safe as we kin. Ain't no point in fergittin' that this here Hatfield could be feelin' kinda mean. Nothin' he'd like better than to bust up a few of us before he lights out.'

Malone did not comment. All he could do was to tell himself that he shouldn't have felt so good so soon.

17

Malone took over from Terpin as soon as they left the office. 'My job,' he said shortly. 'You already did more than your share — you and that stupid friend of yours. Keep an eye on things around here while I ride out and pass the word to Flannery and O'Boyle. I'll use Flannery's men as the guard detail. Denny can send the warning to O'Boyle.'

He had Flannery relieve twenty picked men and send them in for an early supper. Malone explained exactly what he wanted of them. They would work in shifts of five, one man to remain near the office while the other four worked in pairs along the rail line and the wagon road. With four shifts through the night, there shouldn't be any need for sleepiness.

When the men knew the set-up, Malone went on over to the Putnam place for supper. That part had been arranged earlier. The old man had issued the invitations, obviously as a celebration and with some hint that there would be recognition of Terpin's performance in Denver. Malone guessed that the new tension would put a damper on the celebration.

Isabel promptly declared herself on that score. 'This is still a celebration,' she announced when Malone arrived to join Terpin and Flannery as guests. 'We've won. We're going to get this railroad built in spite of everything. I suppose you don't think a woman can feel excited over such a thing — but I do! And I'm not going to worry about any Hatfield or anybody else. So there!'

That started things off on the right foot, and the meal progressed happily. It was only when they were almost ready to leave the table that Malone found himself uneasy. He realized that in the various arguments, serious and otherwise, that had enlivened the meal he had always been on the same side as Isabel Putnam. She had arranged it that way, he felt sure, and the knowledge bothered him. Hearing her frank admission that she had been wrong about Mark Wheeler had been good, but now there was more than a friendly attempt to atone in the way she kept turning to him. He couldn't escape the conclusion that Isabel had decided to like him. It was flattering, but it was something he had to avoid.

It took some of the fun out of things when he turned silent, making it a point to disagree with Isabel when she pressed him or ignoring her when she didn't. He wasn't discourteous, but he knew that the others were reacting to his attitude just as he had reacted to Isabel's enthusiastic approach. He hated to spoil things, but he wasn't going to let matters get out of hand.

The occasion slowed and then halted completely. Isabel abruptly left the room, stating rather lamely that she wished to help her aunt in the kitchen. Then Terpin and Flannery started out. Putnam recovered himself long enough to say, 'You got a bonus comin', Matt. Want it in cash when we get some or would you take stock now?'

'Yuh don't owe me nothin'.' Terpin grinned. 'I'm a stockholder takin' care o' my property. I wouldn't mind ownin' a bit more stock, though.' His round face still managed carry the innocent expression that it had been wearing since his return from Denver.

Putnam laughed. 'I'll take it up with my partner. Seems like it's a matter that can't very well come before the corporation.'

Malone had started to follow the other two men, but the hint was clear. He remained behind, staring hard as he tried to figure out what Putnam's stern glance meant.

'I'll go along on any deal for Terpin,' he said. 'He deserves anything we can give him.'

'That ain't why I wanted to see you alone. Why in hell did you snap Iz off so short this evenin'? Seemed to me like you was gettin' along real good with her and then you changed. I figure she's kinda hurt about it'

'That's the way I intended it. Isabel's a mighty fine girl, Hannibal. I wouldn't want to see her hurt.'

'She's hurt right now.'

'Not much. Not as much as she might be if we got to be friendly and then . . . '

'What in hell are you talkin' about, boy?'

'Kinda obvious, I think. In the last couple of days Isabel has been acting . . . well, like a woman . . . Hell, you know what I mean! I think she likes me. A nice girl like her hasn't got any business getting interested in a man who made a trade out of killing people.'

Putnam looked relieved. 'So that's it! I mighta knowed. Tell me, Malone, did you ever shoot anybody who wasn't on the wrong side of the law?'

'No. But I can't tell myself that I worked for the law because it was the law. It just happened that being a lawman let me put on the kind of stupid show that I wanted to put on. I didn't care any more for the law than I did for the human vermin I had to shoot. Maybe some of those poor devils would be alive right now if I hadn't been so damned proud of myself. I could have argued instead of demanded.'

Putnam waved it all aside. 'Never shot nobody exceptin' in fair fight?'

'No. If you can fight fair when you know you'll win.'

Putnam's expression showed clear disgust. 'There's such a thing as gettin' too damned conscientious, Malone. I ain't sayin' this to tell you what I think you oughta do, not about Iz, anyhow. That ain't none o' my business. But I'm tellin' you that you'd better put the Jack Kyle outa your head just like you put him offa your face. It don't make sense to torment yourself for nothin'.'

Malone spent a sleepless night. Maybe it was the pain in the left elbow. Maybe it was the way he kept listening for trouble outside. Maybe it wasn't either of them. He turned out at dawn, making the rounds of the last-shift sentries and getting their reports. Nothing had happened anywhere in the valley.

Flannery took his work gangs out as usual, only the sentries being relieved for a couple of hours. The day was coming up warm, and there wasn't a cloud in the sky. It seemed to Malone that it was anything but an ominous sort of day, but he couldn't get over the feeling that something was going to happen.

He stopped in at the office after the day was well started getting a casual smile from Isabel. The girl might have been annoyed at him last night, but this morning she was keeping herself well in hand. He exchanged a few words with Putnam and then went out again. The sentries had been taken off post at daybreak, but somebody needed to keep an eye on the valley. The danger was by no means over.

An hour later he went back toward the office as the engine came back to the rail yard with empties. Putnam came out to announce half worriedly, 'I reckon we'd better make the junction trip now, Malone. Sooner we hear what happened last night, the sooner we'll get ourselves off tenterhooks. Flannery can get along with the stuff he's got up there.'

Terpin and Isabel came out of the office to stand behind him, watching as Withers hurried across to give the changed orders to the train crew. 'One of us better make the trip the fat man said. 'No tellin' what could happen along the line.'

'Nothing's going to happen,' Isabel said confidently. 'We've been expecting trouble for so long that we can't get the idea that it's all over.'

'I hope you're right,' Malone told her quietly.

She gave him a quick glance but turned away again, not trying to talk above the noise the little engine was making as it started to pick up a string of empties for the down trip.

It was when the cars were pulled off the siding directly in front of the office that it happened. Suddenly two men appeared from behind a stack of kegs, both with guns leveled. They looked scratched and battered, as though they had spent some rough hours in the woods, but their grim intentions were clear even before Hatfield shouted, 'Nobody makes a move! First try gets a lot of people killed!' Malone took a quick look around. Withers was still up the track. The train crew was with the engine, a dozen car-lengths away. So far as he could tell there was nobody in the office. Hatfield had made his move at just the right time — for him.

The gunman snapped harsh orders as he closed in. 'We're takin' Putnam and the girl as hostages. Get that straight. We want hosses and we want 'em in a hurry. Let's get movin'.'

'Yuh're a damned idjit, Hatfield,' Terpin told him, his voice low. 'Yuh'll never git away with it.'

'Don't give me any gab, blubber-guts! Likely I'll bore a hole in the fat before I leave, but don't make me do it right now. Come on, Putnam. Get started toward them corrals!' He waved his gun in the direction indicated. 'Yuh got yuhr orders, Wick,' he went on. 'Anybody makes a move — shoot the old man. I shoot the girl. Everybody remember that!'

Malone had been doing some fast thinking. It was evident that Hatfield was keeping his closest watch on Terpin. The fat man had his gun slung around his immense waist, and the lean man probably had heard that Matt was no soft touch with a weapon. Malone — his left arm conspicuously bandaged — was being almost ignored. He knew that he could make a move and get away with it, but he didn't dare let Matt be caught unaware.

'You talk too much with your mouth, Hatfield,' Malone said calmly. 'It don't sound good comin' from a man who gets heaved around barrooms.'

There was a split-second in which Hatfield's astonishment kept him silent. Then the red came into his grimy face, and he let his gun waver a little from where it had been menacing Terpin and Putnam. 'Well, if it ain't Lefty Malone with the bum left arm! Talkin' big. All right, mister. I ain't fergettin' that I got a couple o' scores to settle. Mebbe yuh'd like to git yourn right now!'

He had let his anger make him take his eyes from Terpin. Malone knew that the other man was also letting his attention become distracted. This was the time.

'Matt! Get Wick!' he snapped as he went for his gun. Probably Terpin would have gotten the point of the strategy without the cue, but it didn't hurt to yell. Certainly it didn't slow his draw. Two shots crashed almost in unison a second pair following so closely that the roar of the guns sounded like one big noise with a split-second lull in the middle of it. Isabel screamed.

Malone stepped clear of the smoke haze, making sure that neither of the two outlaws would fire again. Then he swung to ask the girl, 'You hurt?'

She shook her head. 'Just acting like a woman. But thanks for asking.' She had recovered in a hurry, her words sounding as cool as though nothing unusual had happened.

For the next few moments Terpin did the talking. He cursed happily as he ran forward with surprising speed to take quick looks at the fallen men. 'Both dead,' he reported. 'Anybody else git it?'

Nobody replied. Putnam didn't seem to have any words and Isabel evidently had spoken hers. Obviously neither of them had been hit. Terpin went back to his inspection of the casualties, leaving Malone to the uneasy certainty that the fat man wasn't going to be fooled any longer.

Withers, the train crew, and a couple of hostlers came up at a run, and there was a flurry of talk, mostly explanations. Terpin took charge once more. 'Might as well make the run to the junction,' he announced. 'Yuh got them empties ready to go. We won't be needin' no word from the lawmen, but I reckon they'll be obliged if we deliver a couple o' dead bandits fer 'em. Load 'em in one o' them gondolas, boys. They ain't goin' to mind it a damned bit.'

At that point Isabel seemed to feel that she had had enough. She had kept her nerve during the crisis and the gun-fight, but the sight of the dead men being dumped into a gondola was more than she could take.

'Better go with her, Hannibal,' Malone suggested. 'She might decide to faint or something.'

'Why don't you go?' the little man said with a sickly grin. 'You're the one saved her.'

'Come off it! Matt came through — again.'

The little man's smile looked a little more natural as he shook his head. 'I saw how it happened. You got Hatfield with your first shot, ruinin' his aim so that his slug went God knows where. Then you got in a second shot at the other man before he knew what happened. Matt fired but he was a shade late.'

'Soon enough,' Malone retorted. 'Wick never got around to shooting.'

'I ain't takin' nothin' away from Matt. It's just that he didn't get his shot in ahead of yours. I wonder if he knows it?'

'Go take care of your daughter,'

Malone told him. 'I might as well talk to Matt. He knows, all right.'

Terpin didn't come near him until the train was out of sight. Then, after he had sent the hostlers back to their jobs, he waddled across to where Malone waited.

'Seems like I wasn't jest imaginin' things,' he greeted. 'Yuh're mebbe faster with yer right hand than yuh was with yer left.'

'Meaning what?'

Terpin grinned. 'Meanin' it's lucky there wasn't more folks around to watch that bit o' gunplay. In no time at all word would be gittin' around that Jack Kyle wasn't dead. Then a whole flock o' cheap gunnies would be tryin' to git him. Like yuh told me once, there's so many fast guns in the country that they git each other killed off mighty fast.'

He watched as Malone's mouth relaxed. Then he added, 'Better slip a fresh shell in one o' them chambers. Then let folks see yuh reload just one. Mebbe they'll figger there was only three shots fired and there won't be no talk about how yuh got two shots off before I could fire one. I reckon none of us is gonna blab about how yuh beat Hatfield when he already had his gun out.'

'Thanks. I'll take your advice.'

'Don't mention it. I kinda owe yuh a bit o' good advice. After all, I took some o' your'n about how to bust up a bank.'

Malone stuck out his hand and the fat man grabbed it. Neither of them said another word. None seemed to be needed.

★ ★ ★

In the cook shack that night, Terpin more than made up for the things he had not said to Malone. The hostlers and the train crew had seen enough from a distance to know that Hatfield and Wick had been holding their prisoners at gunpoint, and they were completely at a loss to understand how Terpin and Malone had managed to buck such odds. Terpin told them.

'This here Lefty Malone is almost as

sneaky as me,' he explained. 'That sonof-abitch Hatfield was mighty cocky. Then Malone asked him if he didn't think he was takin' a hell of a risk to tangle with a cripple and a fat slob. That made the bastard laugh — and the minute he laughed I had him. Malone got in a shot at the other before he knowed what had happened to his boss. Kinda talked 'em out of their wits — and outa the world. Me, I ain't never goin' to listen when that Malone talks; he's dangerous!'

Nobody believed him, but they didn't know what else to believe. When all of the ribald talk was over, the general belief seemed to be that Terpin had pulled a neat bit of gunplay and that Malone had managed to help because the enemy had figured him to be helpless and had ignored him. For Malone that was good enough. He simply finished his supper and headed for his warehouse quarters to pack up his belongings. The job was done; the sooner he got away the better.

He didn't see Terpin again during the evening and the fat man was out on the job at daybreak. He got his breakfast with a minimum of conversation, simply refusing to talk when the cook-shack hands tried to get something out of him. Then he headed toward the office. There was no point in dragging it out.

'I'll be taking the train down to the junction,' be told Putnam when he went in, nodding casually to Isabel but not returning her smile of greeting. 'Seems like you don't need me up here any more. I think I'll just retire and live on my income as a stockholder in mines and railroads.'

The attempted humor didn't get very far. Putnam started to sputter his objections, but his daughter cut him short. 'If you're leaving because you think people are going to start talking about the Jack Kyle days, you might as well stay here. None of us are going to say a word.'

He stammered, caught completely by surprise. 'You know about . . . ? How did you . . . ?'

She gave him her best smile. As he had noted earlier, it was a good one. 'I'm a very good guesser. Remember? I figure things out when I have a few facts to go on. This was quite obvious.'

'What facts?' He was still trying to recover from his surprise.

'Some of the things I've heard and read about a lawman who could use either hand with equal skill. A letter my father wrote to me some years ago about a wounded man who had become his partner. And, of course, your prompt action yesterday. I haven't thanked you yet for saving my life, so this is as good a time as any. Thanks.'

He forced a grin. 'A pleasure. But Matt Terpin . . . '

'Please don't interrupt. I'm not done with my guesses. I am also guessing that you have been rather aloof toward me because you think I might hold your past against you. I don't — particularly after yesterday. Now tell me. Am I a good guesser?'

Old Put exploded. 'Damned if she ain't gettin' as crooked as Terpin! All that talk about guessin'. I told her the whole damned yarn last night.'

'Father!' she protested. 'I thought I could trust you not to spoil it for me!'

'And I thought I could trust him not to talk,' Malone put in. 'He's worse than Terpin. Matt lied like a gentleman to keep my secret for me.'

'You better stick around,' she advised, the smile coming back. 'I think it'll take both of us to watch them.'

Malone nodded, his frown as fierce as it was false. 'And there's another thing, now that we've got around to being stockholders in a going concern. Unless we work together they could outvote us in stockholders meeting.'

'Talk louder and cuss,' Old Put advised. 'You might as well sound like Matt Terpin as think like him.'

'Hah!' Isabel exclaimed. As had happened before, that seemed to end the conversation. For all practical purposes, at least.

We do hope that you have enjoyed reading this large print book.

Did you know that all of our titles are available for purchase?

We publish a wide range of high quality large print books including:
Romances, Mysteries, Classics
General Fiction
Non Fiction and Westerns

Special interest titles available in large print are:
The Little Oxford Dictionary
Music Book, Song Book
Hymn Book, Service Book

Also available from us courtesy of Oxford University Press:
Young Readers' Dictionary
(large print edition)
Young Readers' Thesaurus
(large print edition)

For further information or a free brochure, please contact us at:
Ulverscroft Large Print Books Ltd.,
The Green, Bradgate Road, Anstey,
Leicester, LE7 7FU, England.
Tel: (00 44) **0116 236 4325**
Fax: (00 44) **0116 234 0205**

*Other titles in the
Linford Western Library:*

THE LAWLESS BORDER

Allan Vaughan Elston

It was just one year ago that the O'Hara brothers planned to buy themselves a ranch, settle down, and raise some stock. But that was before Milton disappeared the night after he won forty-four hundred dollars at a poker game. Certain that his brother was hijacked and murdered for his winnings, Lynn vows to investigate. When he arrives in Tucson, there's one man left on his list . . . and he finds himself face-to-face with the ugly muzzle of a six-gun!